"We're sharing
next few hour

Tess paused and gl
secured by his own handcuffs. The man was hard angles of bone and solid muscle, but his crystalline-gray eyes were soft—even beautiful.

"Connor." His interjection was brusque. "Drop the agent part, lady, since the fact that I'm FBI doesn't seem to mean much to you. And yeah, we're in a motel room, but not for any of the reasons a man and woman usually come to a place like this."

She felt faint heat touch her cheeks. Turning her back, she rummaged through her purse. "You sound disappointed, Agent Connor. Although I doubt you have much social life at all. The job's your life. You probably live in a one-bedroom apartment and you've never bothered buying more than a bed and maybe a couch. Did I miss anything?"

"Just that I always carry a spare key for my handcuffs." Spinning around in shock, she saw crystal-gray eyes looking coldly down on her. "Aside from that, I'd say you were dead on, lady. Seeing as you know me so well, this shouldn't be a surprise."

Even as Tess's lips parted in a gasp, Connor's mouth came down hard on hers.

Dear Harlequin Intrigue Reader,

We have a superb lineup of outstanding romantic suspense this month starting with another round of QUANTUM MEN from Amanda Stevens. A *Silent Storm* is brewing in Texas and it's about to break....

More great series continue with Harper Allen's MEN OF THE DOUBLE B RANCH trilogy. *A Desperado Lawman* has his hands full with a spitfire who is every bit his match. As well, B.J. Daniels adds the second installment to her CASCADES CONCEALED miniseries with *Day of Reckoning*.

In *Secret Witness* by Jessica Andersen, a woman finds herself caught between a rock—a killer threatening her child—and a hard place—the detective in charge of the case. What will happen when she has to make the most inconceivable choice any woman can make?

Launching this month is a new promotion we are calling COWBOY COPS. Need I say more? Look for *Behind the Shield* by veteran Harlequin Intrigue author Sheryl Lynn. And newcomer, Rosemary Heim, contributes to DEAD BOLT with *Memory Reload*.

Enjoy!

Sincerely,

Denise O'Sullivan
Senior Editor
Harlequin Intrigue

DESPERADO
LAWMAN
HARPER ALLEN

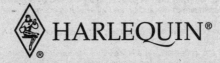
HARLEQUIN®

TORONTO • NEW YORK • LONDON
AMSTERDAM • PARIS • SYDNEY • HAMBURG
STOCKHOLM • ATHENS • TOKYO • MILAN • MADRID
PRAGUE • WARSAW • BUDAPEST • AUCKLAND

ISBN 0-373-22760-4

DESPERADO LAWMAN

ABOUT THE AUTHOR

Harper Allen lives in the country in the middle of a hundred acres of maple trees with her husband, Wayne, six cats, four dogs—and a very nervous cockatiel at the bottom of the food chain. For excitement she and Wayne drive to the nearest village and buy jumbo bags of pet food. She believes in love at first sight because it happened to her.

Books by Harper Allen

HARLEQUIN INTRIGUE
468—THE MAN THAT GOT AWAY
547—TWICE TEMPTED
599—WOMAN MOST WANTED
628—GUARDING JANE DOE*
632—SULLIVAN'S LAST STAND*
663—THE BRIDE AND THE MERCENARY*
680—THE NIGHT IN QUESTION
695—McQUEEN'S HEAT
735—COVERT COWBOY
754—LONE RIDER BODYGUARD†
760—DESPERADO LAWMAN†

*The Avengers
†Men of the Double B Ranch

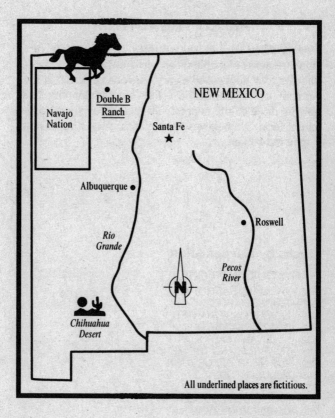

NEW MEXICO

Navajo
Nation

Double B
Ranch

Santa Fe

Albuquerque

Roswell

Rio
Grande

Pecos
River

N

Chihuahua
Desert

All underlined places are fictitious.

CAST OF CHARACTERS

Tess Smith—On the run with a child witness, reporter Tess can't allow FBI Agent Virgil Connor to take Joey back into custody—not when someone in the Agency is a traitor. But hijacking Connor at gunpoint wasn't the plan....

Virgil Connor—Even if Tess Smith is right about Joey, he can't let them stay on the run forever. But can he protect them from an unknown enemy?

Joey Begand—"I see monsters." That's what nine-year-old Joey's been saying since he witnessed a murder. The only adult who believes him is Tess, but can she keep him safe from a killer?

Del Hawkins—The tough ex-marine runs a boot camp ranch for bad boys—like Connor once was. But his own past holds a dark secret that could put Tess and young Joey in danger.

Paula Geddes—Connor's partner, she's already risked her life once to keep witness Joey Begand safe.

John McLeish—Connor wants him for murder. Del remembers him as a hero. Tess wonders if they're both right.

Arne Jansen—The FBI Area Director has no choice but to put out a shoot-to-kill order on now fugitives Agent Connor and Tess.

Alice Tahe—The Navajo matriarch sees evil threatening the Double B Ranch and Joey.

To T.:

Tell the others the circle is unbroken, buddy.

Prologue

When the night-light in his room suddenly went off, Joey Begand knew the killer had done something to the electricity.

He sat up fast in the dark. Swinging his sneaker-clad feet out from the covers, he reached for the duffel bag he'd stashed under the bed the day he'd been brought here, just as if he had been waiting for this moment all along. He had been. He'd even tried to warn the agents guarding him that calling this place a safe house was stupid since it was an apartment, not a house, and hiding here wasn't going to keep him safe at all.

But that was the trouble with being nine years old. Grown-ups thought you didn't know a thing.

He was going to have to get out of here. Then he was going to have to find the one person in the world he figured *could* protect him.

She'd snuck onto a top-secret government base and watched an alien autopsy. She'd tracked Bigfoot and even taken a picture of him—kind of a blurry one, but that was because if she'd gotten any closer Big-foot would have smelled her scent and torn her apart.

She'd hunted down a whole colony of vampires living in the mountains just north of Albuquerque, and if it hadn't been for the crucifix she always wore around her neck she never would have been heard of again.

Tess Smith, star reporter for the *National Eye-Opener,* wasn't like most other grown-ups, Joey told himself shakily. Tess Smith believed in monsters. She went up against them every day—went up against them and whipped their ugly monster butts.

Keeping a little kid safe from the monster who was trying to kill him would be a piece of cake for Tess Smith, nine-year-old federal witness Joey Begand thought desperately as he heard the muffled thud of the first body falling somewhere in the darkened safe house....

Chapter One

FBI Special Agent Virgil Connor pushed open the door of the all-night diner just outside of Roswell, New Mexico.

"Coffee?"

To hell with the heat, caffeine had become a food group over the past few hours, Connor told himself as the waitress plunked a mug in front of him and he slid into a booth adjacent to one occupied by a brunette with a grubby hellion. The waitress plunked a mug in front of him. Out of the corner of his eye he saw the hellion staring at him through an uncut swath of straight, black hair. He lifted his menu, blocking the kid's view.

For two solid days he'd made the rounds of truck stops and diners like this one. The grunt work had just paid off.

The kid was Joey Begand. Connor had no idea who the woman was, but kidnapping a child who just happened to be a federal witness wasn't the only charge she was facing. He could think of a dozen others, starting with accessory to murder. Breaking the news of Bill Danzig's death to the slain agent's wife two nights ago had been the worst moment of his career.

"Keep the ketchup on your side of the plate and stop playing with those fries." The husky-voiced command came from the brunette. "We can't stay here all night, you know."

"Okay, Tess."

Connor risked a glance over the top of his menu. Instead of the suspicious glare he'd favored Connor with, the gaze the urchin was directing at the tight-lipped brunette was wide and shining. Joey picked up a too-large cluster of fries with fingers that were even grubbier than the rest of him.

"That's prob'ly not what it looked like, right, Tess? I betcha they got it all wrong, huh?"

The woman called Tess frowned. "For crying out loud, you don't have to choke on them," she said swiftly. "Put half of those back. Who got what wrong?"

"So what'll it be?"

Connor blinked. The diner's waitress, pencil at the ready, had paused beside his booth. He snapped the menu shut.

"Cheeseburger, plain," he said, coming to a decision that had nothing to do with food. "Is there a phone I can use?"

He needed backup. He would have preferred to keep this takedown low profile, but low profile took second place to the safety of civilians, especially when one of those civilians was a child. There was a chance he could still keep a lid on the situation by using the security of a land line, instead of contacting the Agency office on his cell phone.

"Pay phone's outside." The waitress tucked her pencil behind her ear.

"…nothin' like *them,* right? So what did it really look like, Tess?"

A ketchup-dipped fry in his hand, Joey was pointing to a dangling row of bobble-head dolls suspended over the cash register. About to slide from the booth and head outside to make his call, Connor checked his movement.

The dolls for sale, their spindly bodies topped by teardrop-shaped heads set with jet-black eyes, were an obvious attempt to capitalize on the beyond-the-fringe theory that an alien spaceship had once crashed near Roswell. If the brunette was unbalanced enough to believe in aliens and government cover-ups, she could be even more dangerous than he'd realized.

"How would I know?" The note of impatient confusion in her voice was reassuringly normal, and Connor began to get up from his seat again. "If you're not going to finish those fries I'll eat them. Then we'd better start figuring out how we're—"

She stopped abruptly.

"Oh, yeah, the autopsy in Hangar 61." Sounding weary, she raked slim fingers through short, feather-cut hair. "Well, you saw the secret photographs I took, so you know what it looked like. For one thing, it had three eyes, not just two."

Joey looked thoughtful. "How come they don't get you a better camera, Tess? 'Cause those pictures were a lot like the Bigfoot ones and that photo you took

of Elvis a couple of months ago when you found out
he was still alive and working in a used-car lot—all
blurry and kind of shadowy.''

Connor let his gaze drift past the woman as he
made his way to the door. She didn't look insane. She
looked bone tired, and under her brown eyes—amber-
brown eyes, he noted before they were hidden by the
hand she brought up to massage her temples—were
dark shadows, but she didn't look insane.

Except she had to be. Alien autopsies, Elvis sight-
ings, Bigfoot…replete with photographs, according to
what Joey had just said. She was living in her own
unbalanced universe. A woman who was convinced
she had proof positive that the King hadn't left the
building would have no trouble believing that being
a party to abduction and murder was somehow jus-
tifiable.

What was worse, Joey Begand seemed to have allied himself with his kidnapper. Hoping that the kid
would seize the first opportunity to run from her
wasn't part of the game plan anymore, Connor
thought in frustration as he stepped outside. He
headed around the corner of the building to the pay
phone, his mind racing.

He wasn't worried about being unable to reach the
man he needed to contact. Area Director Jansen
hadn't left his desk since the night the safe house had
been blown, leaving Paula Geddes wounded, Danzig
dead and Rick Leroy, the third agent on duty, gone
without a trace. Leroy had to be allied with the brunette, Connor surmised, lifting the phone's receiver.
The bastard was nervy, all right—that was a given,

since he'd obviously been working against his own people for some time—but even Leroy must have known that once the snatch had gone down every law enforcement officer available would be on the lookout for him.

Leroy also would have guessed that Joey's description wouldn't be as indiscriminately revealed to the media and public as his own, for fear that whoever had the child would panic and eliminate him. He would have figured that if he delegated a woman to escort Joey to wherever it was he wanted the boy, chances were his female accomplice wouldn't run into any problems.

There were two things Leroy hadn't counted on, Connor thought in grim satisfaction. He hadn't counted on a nine-year-old's need for frequent bathroom breaks on a car trip. And he hadn't counted on his girlfriend being soft enough to stop several times to accommodate—

"I'm holding a gun about two inches away from your spine, Agent. Hang up that phone and don't even think of going for your own weapon."

The low warning came from directly behind him, but Connor didn't have to look to know who was delivering it. Her voice didn't suit her, he thought as he carefully set the phone back in its cradle and brought both his hands up to shoulder height. Her pixie haircut and slim build gave her the same street-urchin quality that Joey had, but as soon as she opened her mouth those husky, froggy tones made her sound as if she should be poured into black satin and purring out a torch song in some smoky bar. Slowly he turned around.

She wasn't bluffing. The gun she was holding was a purse-size derringer, but real enough. He decided to try a bluff of his own.

"My wallet's in my back pocket. Not that this mugging's going to make you rich, for God's sake. I'm a plastics salesman, and—"

"Bull." There was scorn in those amber eyes. "You're FBI. Not even the most unsuccessful salesman would pick a suit as bargain basement as the one you've got on. And I bet the polyester shirt you're wearing under that jacket's drip-dry and short-sleeved, right?"

She snorted. "Joey figured you for a Fed as soon as you walked in. I knew he was right when I saw you watching us, Agent. Hand over your gun."

"Or what? You'll whistle up Bigfoot and sic him on me?" Giving up his bluff, Connor shook his head. "This isn't one of your fantasies, lady. This is real life and you're in real trouble. Instead of handing you my gun I'll give you the chance to put yours down, but if you decide not to take me up on my offer you won't leave me much choice."

He began to lower his hands. "I don't think you're going to get off more than one shot, if that. And one bullet's not about to stop me from taking Joey Begand away from you and back into protective—"

"I'm not going back, mister. Did you stop him before he made his phone call, Tess?"

Connor froze, his fingers inches away from his gun. He saw the raw fear that flashed through the amber eyes facing him, saw the derringer in Tess's hand waver.

It would have been the perfect opportunity to make his move and wrest her weapon away from her. But he wasn't going to chance it—not with a small boy only feet away.

"I told you to stay put, Joey." Her voice was as unsteady as her hand, though she didn't take her gaze from him. "Go back into the diner and wait until you see me pull up outside, like we agreed."

"His cheeseburger's ready." Joey sounded as defensive as only a nine-year-old could. "The waitress told the busboy to take out the garbage and see if he was really using the phone or if he'd taken off."

"Joey, listen to me." The last thing he needed was another innocent bystander blundering on to the scene, Connor thought. "Tess isn't your friend. She's working with the person who killed Bill, one of the agents guarding you at the safe house, and who nearly killed Paula, the lady agent who was watching over you that night. My guess is she wants to take you to her partner, and when she does, he's going to kill you."

"Rick double-crossed you guys?" Joey's eyes widened. He met Connor's swift frown and shrugged. "You said Bill was killed and Paula was hurt. I figured since you never said anything about Rick he prob'ly was the one who sold the Agency out."

"Joey, stay out of this. Where's your car parked, Agent?" Tess—the name she'd given to Joey probably wasn't her real one, Connor thought, but it would do for now—bit off the question. "I want you to hand over your weapon real carefully, and then you're going to take us to your vehicle. Mine barely made it off the highway before it died, so we need a ride out of here. Let's start with the gun.''

It was his own fault, Connor told himself, carefully pulling aside his jacket with one hand to reveal his shoulder-holstered automatic and even more carefully withdrawing the weapon. He'd let himself be lulled into complacency by windblown hair and exhausted golden-brown eyes, and he'd paid for that mistake by being bushwhacked. He couldn't remember the last time he'd allowed himself to let down his guard so easily.

Or could he? A stray memory from his past—his distant past, he thought wryly—drifted into his mind as he deposited his gun into her outstretched palm. A run-in with the law when he hadn't been much older than Joey had resulted in him being given the choice of juvenile detention or a year-long stay at what was essentially a boot camp for wayward teens. Run by disabled ex-Marine Del Hawkins, the Double B Ranch had taken in an angry sixteen-year-old street fighter and twelve months later had released a tough and capable young man back into the world.

Del and the Double B had turned his life around. So when the ex-Marine had called on him for his help with a problem the ranch had been facing a month ago, he'd been grateful for the chance to repay even a small part of the debt he owed the man. That time spent on the ranch as a young, reckless teen had taught him a lifetime of lessons.

Don't let that hammer-headed Appaloosa gelding

*fool you, boys. Some days Chorizo looks as harmless
as a little lamb. But he's as tricky as the devil, and
the first time you forget that might be your last.*

Del's drawled warning had been directed at four
know-it-all hell-raisers. California golden-boy Tye
Adams, banished to the Double B by his wealthy father after nearly killing himself on a stolen motorcy-
cle, had been the first to take on Chorizo. Watching
him stumble back behind the safety of the corral bars,
bruised and bleeding, the next kid up, Jess Crawford,
simply shook his head.

"I'm just a computer geek sent here for hacking
into school records," Jess countered. "I never said I
was the macho type, and I don't intend to start now.
You shouldn't, either, Virgil."

Connor had always suspected it had been Jess's use
of his hated first name that had prompted him to get
onto Chorizo's back, but whatever the reason, seconds later he'd found himself landing on hard-packed
dirt, the wind knocked out of him. Even while he'd
been trying to drag some much-needed oxygen into
his burning lungs he'd seen the gelding's razor-sharp
hooves come down inches from his head. Only the
swift intervention of Gabe Riggs, another of the boys,
who'd ducked between the corral's bars and dragged
him to safety, had frustrated the Appaloosa's intentions of making mincemeat out of him.

His run-in with the hammer-headed gelding should
have taught him a lesson, Connor thought now.

Tess wasn't much taller than Joey, and even when
he'd seen her sitting in the diner he'd known his own
solid six-three frame had to top hers by a good twelve

inches or so. But her petiteness wasn't the main reason he'd underestimated the woman now gesturing impatiently at him with his own gun.

Crazy she might be. Vulnerable she wasn't. He wouldn't make that mistake a second time.

"My car's over there," he said tonelessly. "But I'm asking you one last time to give yourself up."

"I can't do that, Agent." Was he fooling himself again, or was there regret in those husky tones? "I can't hand Joey back over to the Agency, and that's final. Now, move."

She'd just sealed her own fate, Connor thought. Prompted by the gun at his back, he headed across the parking lot to his car. He might wish this had turned out otherwise, but there was no reason to feel such desolation at her decision.

He wondered briefly why he did. Then he dismissed the question, knowing he couldn't afford the distraction.

Sometime tonight those amber eyes would close forever, Agent Virgil Connor told himself bleakly. And he was probably going to be the one who would have to kill her.

Chapter Two

She'd kidnapped a federal agent, Tess Smith thought hollowly a few hours later. He was right—this wasn't one of the fantastic stories that ran under her byline in the *National Eye-Opener*. Even if she'd wanted to pretend otherwise, a glance across the motel room at the grim-faced man sitting on a chair and secured by his own handcuffs to the steel bracket bolting down the television set was chilling proof of her actions.

In the bed a few feet away Joey had finally fallen asleep, his tough little face free of all worry for the moment. Beside him was a bobble-head doll from the diner, bought with the change from the money she'd left him to pay for their meal when she'd slipped from their booth to follow the Fed.

She hadn't had the heart to scold him over his unauthorized purchase. The monsters in his young life were all too real. She could understand why a plastic one might bring comfort.

The same need to believe that monsters weren't invincible was obviously why Joey was one of the *Eye-Opener*'s biggest fans. One of *her* biggest fans, rather, Tess corrected herself. Guilt flickered through her, as it had done more than once in the past two days. She didn't know why she hadn't told Joey the truth, since it was something he was going to find out sooner or later, anyway. But maybe it was better that he learn it himself, the way she'd had to.

Oh, not that monsters don't exist, Joey, she silently assured the small sleeping figure in the rumpled bed. *They do. They're really real and I really went up against one, just like in those stories I write. Except I didn't defeat it.*

"It defeated me," she said under her breath, her vision suddenly blurring. "I was your age, and the monster won. No one believed me, either."

"How do you know? I might if you took the trouble to explain, lady."

Startled, Tess jerked her attention to the handcuffed man across the room. She'd allowed him to remove his suit jacket before making him manacle his right wrist to the steel bracket, and even as she looked at him she saw the biceps of his secured arm flex. He gave her a thin smile.

"You want to give it a try?"

"Give what a try?"

She didn't trust him, she thought edgily. She didn't trust him and she didn't like him—or, at least, she didn't like what he represented, and that was close enough. He hadn't spoken at all during the drive to this run-down motel, but she'd had the unsettling conviction that he'd been watching every move she'd made, hoping her attention would flag for just one second.

"Try telling me why you're doing this." He

shrugged. "You seem to think no one would believe you, but you haven't given me a chance to hear you out. In fact, you haven't even told me your name."

Feeling obscurely relieved that he'd evidently misheard her murmured words to the sleeping nine-year-old, Tess narrowed her gaze on him. "Going for the psychological approach, Agent? Trying to make me think we could be buddies? Don't waste your breath. Your little ploy's not going to lull me into uncuffing you and handing you back your gun."

She shook her head. "Besides, you know darn well who I am. Even if you don't think too highly of my work, you've obviously read an example of it, since you knew about the Bigfoot story."

Dark eyebrows drew together in a frown. "You're some kind of writer? Sorry, lady, I'm afraid I've never—"

"Oh, please," she snapped. "If I believed everyone who told me they never buy the *Eye-Opener,* I'd figure we have a circulation of about twelve readers in the whole country. The most you'll admit is that you might have glanced at it in a checkout line at the grocery store, right?"

"The *Eye-Opener?*"

He didn't seem to realize he was matching his actions to his flatly phrased comment. The rest of the man was hard angles of bone and solid slabs of muscle, Tess noted incongruously, but his eyes were—

His eyes were beautiful, she thought a heartbeat later. They were a crystalline gray in the tan of his face, fringed with dark, spiky lashes any female would kill for.

She watched as they closed briefly, the lashes dipping to fan against hard ridges of cheekbone. When they opened again she was sure she saw wry humor light them just for a moment.

"You're a tabloid reporter." She hadn't been wrong about the humor. A corner of his mouth quirked upward before it firmed into a straight line once again. "So there wasn't any alien autopsy in Hangar 93?"

She glanced at a fast-asleep Joey before replying. "Hangar 61. But no, of course it wasn't real." She looked at him in confusion. "For heaven's sake, do you think I'm some kind of—"

Belated comprehension flooded through her. "Dear God, you did, didn't you? You thought I was a wacko, crazy enough to be working with whoever's targeting Joey."

She stared coldly at him. "Nice theory, Agent. Too bad it's even less grounded in facts than the stories the *National Eye-Opener* runs every week."

"Connor." His tone was as clipped as hers. "And I don't want to make you think we could be buddies, I'm just tired of being called Agent. Is Tess your real name or is that something else you've let Joey believe?"

"Tess is my real name." When she was annoyed, her voice was raspier than normal, she knew. "Tess Smith. Connor what?"

"Connor's my last name." He grimaced. "These cuffs are cutting off my circulation. How about loosening them?"

"Let me suggest an *Eye-Opener* headline for that

one," she retorted. "FBI Discovers Woman Dumber Than Dirt—She Believed Me When I Said I Wouldn't Try To Escape, Agent Says. The cuffs stay. What's your first name?"

He looked away. "Virgil," he muttered. "But I go by Connor."

His comment a moment ago had stung. She arched an eyebrow. "You think I deliberately lied to Joey, don't you, Virgil? You think I encouraged his hero-worship for my own ends. Is that how you figure it, Virge?"

The eyes she'd thought so beautiful took on a hard glitter. Restlessly Connor—no, *Virgil,* she told herself defiantly—shifted position on the hard wooden chair.

"I still figure you that way, lady. What your day job is doesn't really change anything." He exhaled, his gaze on hers.

"Did Rick Leroy tell you why Joey Begand was being held in an Agency safe house?" He didn't wait for her answer. "It was because he witnessed a murder in an Albuquerque alleyway—the murder of a retired FBI agent, Dean Quayle. Quayle's killer, a homeless man by the name of John MacLeish, was wounded during the encounter, but not badly enough to prevent him from escaping later that night from the hospital where he'd been taken after the police had arrived on the scene. The police found Joey hiding in a Dumpster, his memory of exactly what happened temporarily erased. The doctors say Joey's amnesia won't last."

His tone hardened. "I don't care what your relationship with Leroy is, except for the fact that you have to be working with him, since he handed Joey over to you. What I do want to know is, what was Leroy's deal with Quayle's killer, MacLeish?''

He'd already judged her and found her guilty, Tess thought. She'd gone into this realizing that no explanation she could give would be believed by the authorities. That was why she hadn't bothered to present her side of the story to him during the drive here, and why even now she suspected it was going to be futile to try to make Agent Virgil Connor, a man who obviously lived and breathed his job, understand.

But for a split second she'd thought she'd glimpsed a very different man from the single-minded enforcer of the law he appeared to be. Wasn't it possible that those crystal-gray eyes might see she'd had no other choice but to keep faith with Joey Begand, even if keeping faith meant breaking the law?

It was worth a try. Even before Connor had found them she'd had serious doubts that she could pull this off all by herself.

''Maybe it's time we got a few things straight.'' She paused, wondering how best to present her story. ''First, I don't know what the connection is between Leroy and MacLeish, for the simple reason that I'm not working with Leroy. I've never even met the man, so—''

''For God's sake, woman, save yourself!'' Abruptly the big man stood, the chair he'd been sitting on sliding backward across the linoleum floor. He started to take a step toward her, only to be jerked to a halt by the cuff on his left wrist. ''I don't want to fire the shot that takes you down or stand by and watch another agent have to kill you. But that's the way it's going to happen if you don't call a stop to this.''

Unsteadily Tess got to her feet, the fear she'd been trying to suppress for the past two days spilling over. ''I'm telling you the *truth*, dammit! I'm not working with a killer and I'm not working with a dirty agent. My only loyalty is to a little boy who came to me believing I could keep him safe. That's why I can't bring myself to tell Joey the stories I write are all lies—because he *needs* them to be true. I'm his only hope, and I don't intend to let him down.''

''He came to you?'' There was hostile disbelief in his tone. ''There's no way Joey could have escaped from Leroy after he'd snatched him from that safe house. Try again.''

''Leroy didn't get the chance to snatch him,'' she snapped. ''Joey knew the Agency wouldn't be able to protect him, and the day he arrived at the safe house he started planning how he was going to escape when the time came. He got out through an air duct.''

She took a deep breath. ''Ask him yourself when he wakes up. It's a more hair-raising story than any of my so-called exploits, believe me. Apparently he climbed onto a wardrobe and slid aside a duct panel he'd loosened days before. He hoisted himself up, re-placed the panel, and when he found himself over a nearby vacant apartment he simply dropped down again, courtesy of a knotted length of bedsheet he had ready in his knapsack. Then he took the service stairs to a back exit and trekked across town on foot to my place.''

"Supposing I believe any of that, why did he come to you?" His gaze was unreadable. "Did he know you?"

"He knew of me." She smiled crookedly. "He knew I kicked ugly monster butt, as he put it. Apparently before his mom died last year she was an *Eye-Opener* fan, and Joey told me I was her favorite writer on the paper. I'm sure she wasn't gullible enough to swallow the Hangar 61 and Bigfoot stories, but her son did. He figured since he had a monster to slay, he needed a monster slayer. So he looked me up in the phone book and showed up on my doorstep."

"A monster to slay?" He frowned. "Forget that for the moment. Maybe I can understand why a nine-year-old boy might think a tabloid reporter could protect him better than the FBI, but how the hell did you convince yourself that going on the run with him was a good idea? And where did you intend to take him, anyway?"

"To the Dinetah, of course. I didn't want to go there directly, in case we were being followed." At his blank look, she elaborated. "The Navajo Nation. Joey's mother always made sure he knew his heritage through her was Dineh, as we Navajo call ourselves." She saw his assessing glance at her. "That's right. I'm Dineh, too, Agent."

"Your background isn't what concerns me." With his free hand the big man rubbed his jaw. "But there was nothing in Joey's file to indicate he had any tribe affiliation. If the state authorities had known, when his mother died he would have been put into a facility where his culture would have been emphasized while he was waiting for adoption or fostering.''

''I'm not surprised he didn't tell them. He's a pretty close-mouthed little guy until he gives his trust.''

''And you say he gave his trust to you,'' Connor said shortly. ''I'd like to believe you. Hell, I halfway do, at that. But even if Joey thinks he's safe with you, you know that protecting him is our job, not yours. He isn't being chased by a monster, he's being hunted by a killer, probably two, if MacLeish and Leroy are working together.''

He still didn't get it, Tess told herself wearily. He never would, and she'd been a fool to hope otherwise. Virgil Connor was defined by his badge and his gun. He played by the rules. He didn't think outside the box, and he'd probably get to be area director with those qualities.

Worst of all, he didn't believe in monsters. And that meant he was no protection at all for Joey Begand.

She pushed a stray strand of hair back from her forehead. She intended to be on the road again before sunup, and she desperately needed some sleep before the several hours of driving still ahead of her.

Agent Connor was going to get some shut-eye, too, she thought, which was why she'd had no qualms about informing him about her plans. By the time he awoke tomorrow and found himself alone here, Joey would be on Navajo Nation land where the FBI would need warrants and special permission from tribal leaders to retrieve him—permission she was almost certain wouldn't be forthcoming.

Letting his witness and the woman who'd abducted him slip through his fingers wasn't going to look good on his file, but a blot on Agent Connor's copybook wasn't her biggest worry. Setting the gun down on the dresser beside her, she retrieved her purse from the foot of the bed.

"If your main concerns are MacLeish and Leroy, I'm surprised you aren't out hunting them," she said evenly. "But there's no point in discussing our differing viewpoints, Agent Connor. Whether either one of us likes it or not, we're sharing a motel room for the next few hours, so let's—"

"Connor." His interjection was brusque. "Just Connor. Drop the agent part, lady, since the fact that I'm FBI doesn't seem to mean too much to you. I'm the man you're holding at gunpoint. You're the woman I let pull a fast one on me. Yeah, we're in a motel room, but not for any of the usual reasons a man and woman usually come to a place like this."

Tess felt faint heat touch her cheeks. He was trying to get her off balance, she thought in chagrin. He was succeeding, and although she didn't really understand why his dismissive reference to a sexual tryst should make her color up like an embarrassed schoolgirl, if he got the impression his captor wasn't as tough as she was pretending to be, he might begin to wonder if she'd really use the gun she'd been holding on him.

She'd been wondering that, too.

"You sound disappointed." She allowed a thin smile to curve her lips. "That we're not here for the usual reasons, I mean. I should have guessed a man who dresses the way you do would have a social agenda that revolved around cheap motel rooms.''

His answering smile was just as controlled as hers. ''And I should have guessed that a woman who dreams up stories about Bigfoot wouldn't have any trouble fantasizing about my sex life. Good thing we'll never actually do the dirty together for real, honey. I doubt I'd be able to measure up to what you've probably been imagining about me.''

Outrage flickered swiftly through her. ''Believe me, my imagination wasn't coming up with anything very exciting,'' she retorted. ''In fact, I was probably giving you too much credit. I seriously doubt you have a social life at all.''

She tipped her head to one side. ''Let's see how close I get, okay? The job's your life. You live in a one-bedroom apartment, and you've never bothered buying more than a bed and maybe a couch. You don't have any pictures up on the wall, and those walls are whatever color the previous tenant left them. Am I warm?''

He didn't answer her. Turning her back to him, she rummaged around in her purse for the sleeping pills she was going to have to force him to take. She went on, trying to mask her sudden apprehension with abrasiveness.

''You've got six other white shirts just like the one you're wearing now—short-sleeved and polyester, because they're practical and you don't care how you look as long as you're presentable. You don't know the names of your co-workers' spouses. You volunteer to work Christmas. You get to the gym at least three times a week. Did I miss anything?''

"Just that I always carry a spare key for my handcuffs.''

His voice came from directly behind her. Spinning around in shock, she saw crystal-gray eyes looking coldly down on her, saw the automatic she'd taken from him at the diner firmly gripped in one big hand.

"Aside from that, I'd say you were dead-on, lady,'' he said harshly. "So seeing as you know me so well, this part shouldn't be a surprise, either.''

Even as Tess's lips parted in a gasp, Virgil Connor's mouth came down hard on hers.

Chapter Three

It wasn't a kiss. It was a storm, a hurricane, a lightning strike that immediately shorted out every last electrical impulse in all her nerve endings at once, but it wasn't a kiss. Virgil Connor didn't know how to kiss, Tess thought disjointedly. He probably didn't know how to make love. All the man knew was raw sex.

But he knew everything there was to know about that.

One big hand was spread wide against the back of her head. His other arm was hanging loosely at his side. He was making it clear that if she wanted to she could pull away from him easily enough.

She swayed toward him. Connor shifted his stance automatically, his hand spreading wider and his fingers beginning to slide through her hair as he moved in closer. Through her own half-closed lashes she saw his—dark and thick, drifting down to shut off that brilliant gray gaze.

Suddenly she felt him stiffen. He lifted his head and took a step back, his hand falling from her.

Tess blinked. The next moment appalled horror

raced through her, and she took a stumbling step backward herself. Something flashed behind the mirrored gray of his eyes. A muscle moved tightly at the side of his jaw as he spoke.

"That's one for the books." His tone was flat and dead. "You'd better report me for this when they take you in. I won't contest your statement."

Her mouth felt so swollen and hot she had the impulse to bring her fingertips to her lips. "Why?" Her voice came out in a croak. She tried again, putting more force behind her words. "Why did you do that?"

"I don't know. But it won't happen again." He began to turn away. "I'm going to call my area director and have him send someone to escort—"

"No!" Incautious fury spilled through her at his dismissal of the situation he'd created. She grabbed his arm, noticing as she spun him back to face her that the muscle beneath her grip was rigidly hard. "You're going to tell me what just *happened* here, for God's sake!"

Suddenly remembering Joey, she cast a swiftly contrite glance in the direction of the bed. He was obviously too deeply asleep for anything short of an earthquake to rouse him, but she lowered her tone nonetheless.

"Is it how you get off, Agent Connor?" With a shaky hand she pushed a stray curve of hair off her cheek. "Do you try something like this with all of the women you flash your badge at, or did you just figure you'd give it a shot with me?"

She tightened her grip on his wrist. "You'd better

believe I'd report you if I had any intention of letting you take me in, but I don't. I'm leaving here with Joey, and the only way you can stop me is by using that gun you're holding. My opinion of you right now isn't the greatest, but I don't think you can bring yourself to shoot an unarmed woman.''

Releasing him abruptly, she picked up her purse from the dresser beside them and stalked over to Joey's backpack, on the floor beside the bed. She bent stiffly and grabbed one of its straps, but as she lifted it the flap opened and the contents of the bag tumbled out onto the floor.

Tess squeezed her eyes shut against the sudden prickling of tears she could feel behind her lashes. They were tears of anger and frustration, she told herself. They weren't tears of fear or worry. This wasn't working out the way she'd planned, but in a few minutes she could still be on her way with Joey. In a couple of hours they would be on Navajo Nation land, where Virgil Connor's bullying tactics would slam up against a solid wall of red tape when he attempted to—

''I'm not going to shoot you, Tess.'' He didn't sound bullying, he just sounded tired. ''For what it's worth, it won't come to that and you know it. Look at me.''

She ignored him. Squatting down on her heels, she began to gather up the collection of small-boy treasures that had fallen from Joey's backpack, replacing them as carefully as she could manage with her trembling fingers.

There was a dog-eared collection of baseball cards,

held together by a doubled-over elastic band. Joey was obviously a baseball nut like she was, Tess thought, trying to distract herself from the man standing silently beside her. It would be something they could talk about on the drive ahead of—

"Look at me, Tess."

There was a reluctantly hard note in his tone. Her fingers closed around a carefully folded piece of paper before she unwillingly raised her eyes to his.

"Don't bother." Despair washed over her. "I know what you're going to say."

A muscle moved in his jaw. "I'd better say it anyway, just so we're clear here. I'm a big man. You're what…five-three? Five-four?"

"Three," she answered him tonelessly. "I get it, all right?"

He went on as if she hadn't spoken. "I wouldn't even have to try, Tess. But I don't want it to go down that way and I don't think you do, either. Hand me the car keys."

He needed the keys because she'd left her own gun locked in the glove box. Tess understood he wasn't going to let this situation get out of control again.

That was what Virgil Connor was all about, she realized. He liked well-defined boundaries, smooth-running operations, everything falling into place the way it should. He could react to the unexpected, the illogical, but his immediate response was to bring it back under control, which made his actions with her a moment ago all the more inexplicable. Despite her accusations, she knew instinctively he'd crossed a line with her that he'd never crossed before in his life.

And that knowledge was supremely unimportant. All that mattered was that she'd failed a small boy who'd thought she could protect him. She looked at the paper in her hand, recognizing it for what it was before she began unfolding it.

"They're in my purse," she said flatly. "Get them yourself."

In the creased newspaper photo she was dressed in some kind of pseudo-camouflage outfit and standing in a desert. The wonders of computer graphics, she thought briefly. The picture had been taken in the *Eye-Opener*'s parking lot, her figure superimposed against a generic desert scene later on. The tabloid's photo-tech had also punched up the Rambo-like smeared grease under her eyes and the fake blood soaking one arm of her fatigues to a brilliant red, probably because it had looked too much like the ketchup it was.

The surrounding article had been torn off. Joey likely knew it by heart anyway, she thought.

"Is that you?"

Tess hadn't even noticed that he'd hunkered down beside her to retrieve her purse. She let him take the picture from her.

"No, that's not me." She began to gather up the rest of the scattered odds and ends that had fallen from the backpack. "That's who Joey thinks I am, but that's not me."

"What are you supposed to be doing here?"

Under the bed was another photograph facedown, this one not a clipping from the tabloid but a tiny photo-booth snapshot that must have originally been attached to a strip of pictures. She reached past him for it.

"I'm covered in blood so I guess I'm supposed to be taking a breather after going up against Bigfoot or a mutant lizard or something," she replied curtly. "You said you were going to tell your area director to send someone out. Will Joey and I be riding back to Albuquerque in different vehicles?"

"That's correct procedure." Out of the corner of her eye she saw him shrug. "You're my arrest. He's my witness. I've pulled enough stupid plays tonight without adding to them by transporting the two of you in the same car."

He looked away. "And if I could take back just one of the mistakes I've made since spotting you in that diner it would be the way I moved in on you a few minutes ago. I behaved like a jerk. If you're wondering whether I'm going to be the one taking you in, don't worry, I'll hand you over to the agents Jansen dispatches when they come."

He got to his feet. "I'll make that call now."

"That's not why I asked." Still clutching the second photo, she stood, too. "Can you give me some time alone with Joey? Just a few minutes, that's all I need."

Dark brows drew together. "What for?"

"To tell him he was wrong about me," she said unsteadily. "I owe him that much, Connor. Joey Begand came to me thinking I was someone I'm not, and I should have set him straight right away. Instead, I let him go on believing in a bunch of faked photos and stories, and told myself I was doing it for him."

She lowered her gaze. Aimlessly she turned over the small picture in her hand. ''It's too long and dreary a story to get into, but it's more likely I was doing it for myself. I think I needed to believe that for once in my life I could—''

The breath in her lungs suddenly vanished, taking with it the rest of her unfinished sentence. A giant fist wrapped around her heart and squeezed, tighter and still more tighter. Her hand shaking, Tess brought the tiny photo up until it was only inches from her face.

It couldn't be, she thought in shock. It just *couldn't* be—life didn't operate that way. Connor was right, she'd been living in the *Eye-Opener*'s fantasy world for so long that she'd lost touch with reality. Coincidences this colossal were reserved for the outlandish stories she dreamed up, not for—

It wasn't a coincidence at all. It was why Joey's mother had read everything she'd written, she realized, her throat closing in pain, why Darla Begand— *so that was the name she'd taken,* Tess thought achingly—had made Tess Smith out to be a hero to her small son. It had been the only connection Darla been capable of making with a past she'd tried to blot out.

''I can't leave you alone with Joey, but I'll let you explain things to him.'' Connor was watching her. ''He's a kid, Tess. He'll get over it the way kids do when they find out there's no Santa Claus or Easter Bunny, for crying out loud. Right now you should be worrying about yourself. You've convinced me that you didn't have anything to do with Leroy and what happened at the safe house, but you're still facing serious charges. Kidnapping a child's the worst of them.''

''Not if I had the right to take Joey. Not if I was his guardian, for all intents and purposes.''

Tess met his eyes and saw the impatience, quickly suppressed, that flickered through them. Connor's lips tightened, and when he spoke, some of the harshness he'd previously displayed had crept back into his tone.

''But you're not. Like I was saying, you should be thinking about calling a lawyer. Do you have—''

He bit off his words with a muttered oath and his hand shot out to grab hers as she reached down for her purse. She drew swiftly back.

''I'm not going for a weapon, Agent Connor. I need to show you something.''

''I don't think so.'' The brief humanity he'd shown a few minutes ago had gone. In its place was distrust. ''I let those amber eyes of yours lull me into letting my guard down once already. I won't make that mistake again.''

''My eyes are plain brown, for heaven's sake.'' She pressed her lips together. ''If you're worried I've got a weapon stashed in here, then you get my wallet out for me. It…it's important,'' she added. ''I think you're going to want to see this before you make that call to your director.''

She let go of her purse. He narrowed his gaze assessingly at her. ''All right. I'll let you show me whatever it is you think is so important, and then you stop stalling and allow me to make my call without having to keep a gun trained on you every second. Deal?''

"Deal." She bit her lip as he extracted a leather wallet from the jumble of junk in her purse. "Open it. Pull out the plastic photo protector under the flap.''

He complied and handed the small sheaf of photos to her. In return she handed him the tiny one from Joey's backpack.

"That's Joey and his mom," she said. "I guess she didn't have the money for a department-store portrait, so she had their pictures taken together in one of those booths.''

"Yeah, it looks like. His hair's slicked down, and she obviously arranged the two of them in a pose before she activated the camera," Connor agreed.

He glanced at the curled-up figure in the bed beside them. "From what I know of his background, he's already had more than his share of rough knocks, poor kid. His father was killed in a car accident before he was born, and his mother apparently couldn't seem to keep even the menial jobs she occasionally found. He pretty much grew up on the street. When she died and he was put into the system, he kept hanging around his old haunts, like the alleyway where he saw Mac-Leish kill Quayle.''

He held the photo out to her. "It's always better when family can step in and take over the responsibility for a child, instead of them being shoved into an already overloaded system. Too bad Joey wasn't one of the lucky ones.''

"Joey's luck just changed." Tess didn't take the picture he was holding, but instead slipped one from her wallet. "Everything just changed, Agent. This is a picture of me and my sister, the last one taken of us together. She ran away when I was nine and she was seventeen. Years later I tried to find her, but I never learned what had happened to her."

She swallowed, and forced her next words past the lump in her throat. "Until now."

She handed him the photo from her purse. She saw his gaze sharpen, saw him glance from one picture to the other. He looked up from the two photos to her and she nodded.

"That's right, Joey's my nephew. His mom was my sister. I...I guess Darla's monsters got her in the end," she said unevenly. "I'm not going to let that happen to her son."

Through her tears she stared at him. "Whatever authority the FBI thought they had before Joey's aunt showed up, I'm the one keeping the monsters away from him now."

Chapter Four

"Even if it was my decision to make, I couldn't let you waltz out of here with a federal witness just because you say you're Joey's aunt."

Raking a hand through his hair, Connor turned from the woman sitting on the edge of the bed and moved restlessly to the window, something he'd found himself doing with increasing frequency since Tess had discovered the photo she seemed to think clinched her claim to Joey. Despite the heated discussion they'd been engaged in since, he still hadn't been able to make her understand that her position hadn't changed to any great degree—certainly not enough to have stopped him from phoning Area Director Arne Jansen with the news that the boy had been found.

At the end of the line of units a single light was burning in the motel's office, but otherwise the darkness outside was undisturbed. He hadn't expected the two backup agents Jansen was sending to have arrived yet. He'd just needed a break from the angry gaze Tess was lasering at him. He turned to face her again.

"I agree the Agency fumbled the ball in guarding

Joey, but I promise we won't slip up again. If you care for your nephew at all, you have to see that professionals can protect him from a couple of killers better than one untrained woman could.''

''But as you say, your team of professionals has performed pretty poorly so far.'' Abruptly Tess stood, shooting a glance at the sleeping child in the bed she'd just risen from. ''And you can't protect him from an enemy you don't even know about.''

Her words were barely audible, as if she was of two minds whether or not she wanted him to hear. Connor frowned.

''Just what does that mean?''

Her back to him, she was gathering the few articles she'd earlier set on the dresser, but he guessed that her task was no more valid than his glance out the window had been. She was avoiding his eyes, or trying to. Unfortunately for her every nuance of her expression was caught in the dresser mirror in front of her, and with a start Connor realized the emotion shadowing her features wasn't fear.

It was terror. And terror was far too strong a reaction to have anything to do with his call to Jansen.

In the diner he'd been briefly convinced that Tess Smith was unbalanced. She wasn't, he knew now. Her actions over the past two days might have been rash and poorly thought out, but she'd been well aware of the risks she was running and the consequences of what she was doing. She hadn't known then that Joey was her nephew, so why had she chosen to take those risks and damn those consequences?

It was a question he should have asked himself before, Connor told himself. Why hadn't he?

Because you've been too busy replaying that kiss you forced on her in your mind, a voice inside his head jeered.

"What do you mean, I can't protect Joey from an enemy I don't know about?" With an effort he shut off the jeering voice. "Did he see someone that night at the safe house? Is there a third person working with Leroy and MacLeish?"

Under the white tee she was wearing her shoulders tensed. "I've already told you Joey didn't see anyone the night he escaped, and he's still blanking out when he tries to remember exactly what happened between MacLeish and the retired agent who was killed in that alleyway. It's too bad the Agency's doctors didn't take the time to find out what caused Joey's mind to take refuge in a temporary amnesia."

He was getting tired of talking to the back of her head, Connor thought impatiently. Between the white of her shirt and the silky black strands of her tousled haircut the nape of her neck seemed disarmingly vulnerable, for some reason.

He scowled. "The shock of seeing a man killed caused his amnesia. The on-site evidence, plus the fact that MacLeish was badly wounded himself, indicated that Quayle didn't go down without a fight. Watching a violent struggle end in murder isn't something any nine-year-old should have to go through."

"I agree. But that wasn't the first time Joey had witnessed violence." Finally she turned to face him, her expression closed. "He's not Beaver Cleaver,

Connor. He hasn't been protected from the seamier side of life, the way children should be. From what Joey's told me, Darla did her best by him while she was battling her own demons, but he'd seen street fights before, even if they'd never resulted in murder.''

Her mouth tightened. ''This is probably going to sound just as crazy to you as the Hangar 61 story. Have you ever heard of something—'' her gaze wavered ''—or some*one,* called Skinwalker?''

Earlier this evening his thoughts had gone to the year he'd spent at the Double B Ranch so long ago—the year he'd been thoroughly humiliated by Chorizo, the year a tough but compassionate Del Hawkins had turned his life around. But Tess's unexpected question brought back his most recent visit to the ranch and the unsettling events that had threatened the Double B just over a month ago.

Those events had eventually been proven to have been orchestrated by an ex-con named Jasper Scudder, but even Del's normally hardheaded composure had been disturbed by the warnings of Navajo matriarch Alice Tahe, who'd predicted that the evil spirit her people called Skinwalker had been behind Scudder's actions…and that although Scudder had perished, the presence of Skinwalker still threatened the Double B and Del.

With no disrespect intended toward either the old lady or her traditional beliefs, Connor thought now, he just didn't buy into the existence of a supernatural big bad. So when Alice Tahe had spoken about a thing that walked like a man, talked like a man, but was all the darkness from the beginning of the world personified, he'd dismissed her Skinwalker as merely one of the myths of the Navajo people.

From her tone, he got the feeling Tess didn't. A slight impatience rose up in him.

"Yeah, I've heard the legend. Why?"

Something sparked behind the amber of her eyes. "Because that's who I'm protecting Joey from, Agent. You might believe he's in danger from Mac-Leish or Leroy, but Joey's convinced Skinwalker's the one who wants him dead. And although I wasn't brought up in the Way—the Navajo Way," she added in explanation, "I'm Dineh enough to think he could be right."

The spark in her gaze fanned to a tiny flame, and color lent a wild-rose tinge to the cinnamon of her skin.

"Don't you get it yet? He doesn't remember what happened between Quayle and MacLeish because everything else was blotted from his mind when he was almost killed himself. I don't know if there was a third person at the safe house the night of the ambush...but there was a third presence in the alleyway the day Quayle was murdered. Joey swears it was Skinwalker. And he says that just before the police showed up, Skinwalker started toward the Dumpster where he was hiding to kill him."

"Skinwalker," Connor repeated. "We're talking about the Navajo Skinwalker, right? An evil ghost, uses his shapeshifting powers to take on the form of a man or a wolf or whatever he wants?" He glanced at the small sleeping form in the bed and then back

at her. "I guess it's possible a kid might see him as
the bogeyman, if he'd been told stories about him in
the past, but encouraging him in that belief—"

"Is that your theory?" Her gaze darkened. "Joey
translated his terror at witnessing Quayle's murder
into something a nine-year-old could understand—a
monster, just like the ones other children see hiding
behind a half-open closet door?"

"Or just like the ones you make a living writing
about," Connor agreed, not bothering to soften the
edge in his voice.

Now it made sense, he thought, annoyed with himself for not figuring it out before. Now he knew why
she'd risked going on the run with the boy long before
she'd discovered there was a family connection between them. He didn't know who he felt angrier at—
her, for turning out to be the journalistic equivalent
of a conartist, or himself for not seeing from the start
what she was up to. Hell, for all he knew maybe she'd
somehow faked that photo she'd conveniently found
in her purse.

"That's what all this was leading to, wasn't it? You
hoped you could get a *National Eye-Opener* front
page out of this, complete with you in your ghost-
busting gear facing down some guy in a monster cos-
tume. Lady, whatever hare-brained notion you've got
of parlaying a federal investigation into journalistic
glory for yourself—"

"Journalistic glory?" The pink in her cheeks flared
to bright patches of anger. "In a rag like the *Eye-
Opener* that gets shoved between the milk and eggs
in a sack of groceries? I'm not *that* delusional, Agent,

and even if I were I wouldn't use a child's fear to my own advantage.'' Her voice shook. ''Believe me, I know how damaging that can be.''

Her vehemence rang too true to have been put on for his benefit, Connor thought. And behind it was something else—something that held an echo of pain and guilt.

But he'd allowed himself to be distracted by Tess Smith's seeming vulnerability once already, he reminded himself. Any pain he thought he detected in her voice wasn't his concern.

''Let's say you didn't intend to use this in one of your stories.'' He shrugged. ''What does that leave me with—that you really believe Joey saw an evil spirit in that alleyway?''

''I told you you'd think it was crazy.'' Her gaze was shuttered. ''But yes, if Joey says Skinwalker's after him, that's enough for me. He needs to know someone's on his side.''

As she spoke, Connor was half-convinced he could feel the warmth of her breath on his own lips, could discern the faintest scent of cloves and carnations coming from her. There was no good reason why he kept thinking of flowers when he looked at Tess Smith, he thought in irritation.

Besides, his involvement with the woman had begun with her leveling a gun at him. If he needed a botanical reference to compare her to, a cholla cactus was probably his best bet—wild fuchsia blossoms behind a formidable barricade of thorns.

But neither her prickliness nor his own inappropriate musings were enough to completely distract him from the care she'd taken in framing her answer to his last question. He knew with sudden certainty what she was trying to hide.

"You don't believe in any of this, either, do you?" He frowned. "You said you weren't brought up in the Way. Admit it—Skinwalker's nothing more than a dim folkloric tradition to you, like the kelpies my Irish grandmother used to tell me about were to me."

"He's real to Joey." She bit off the words. "And despite my sketchy knowledge of my own heritage, I have more respect for the old stories than to dismiss them completely."

"Maybe, but you're standing by Joey for your own reasons, not because you think there's any possibility he's telling the literal truth." He narrowed his gaze on her. "Why is it so important to you that he doesn't go back into protective custody? Is there another threat to him you're not telling—"

Connor broke off abruptly. From the parking lot outside had come the solid *thunk* of a car door closing, and even as he strode to the window he heard a second *thunk*. He pushed the drapes aside and saw an unmarked sedan almost identical to his own, two men standing by it in neatly unobtrusive suits and with expressions of grim alertness as federal issue as their car.

He let the curtain fall closed. "Your ride's here," he said shortly. "When you get to Albuquerque, take my advice and don't count on Area Director Jansen cutting you as much slack as I have. You should have come clean with me from the start."

"I've come as clean with you as I can, Agent Connor. I know you don't accept that, but it's true."

Tess bit into her lower lip. She shook her head, her gaze searching his.

"The thing is, Virgil, I think you do believe in monsters," she said slowly. "You just can't admit it, because if you did your world wouldn't be controllable anymore. What happened that made you build that rigid box around yourself? Did you go up against them once and lose?"

His first impression of her had been correct, Connor told himself tightly, slipping his gun into his shoulder holster. The woman was more than a little out of touch with reality.

"I don't see operating on logic and reason as being boxed in," he grated. "Which is why I'm not the one who's going to have to tell a nine-year-old boy that I'm not the person I let him think I was," he added.

He regretted his comment even before he saw the suddenly stricken look in her eyes. "Sorry, that wasn't necessary," he muttered. "Whatever I thought when I first saw you with Joey, you've convinced me that you only wanted to—"

"No, you're right." The husky tones came out unevenly. "I shouldn't have acted as impulsively as I did. I should have thought things out more logically, like you say."

She was finally beginning to see the light. Connor felt obscurely relieved. Her attitude would be a deciding factor in Jansen's decision whether or not to—

"I should have stayed away from the highways and stayed on the back roads." She exhaled sharply.

"Dammit, I should have taken Joey up on his suggestion to show me how to hotwire a car in that diner parking lot when mine broke down. We would have been long gone by the time you got there."

She hadn't seen the light. She was never going to see the light. Her stubborn defiance was going to land her behind bars, he thought angrily. And it wasn't his problem anymore.

"I would have caught up with you sooner or later." Two sets of footsteps were approaching along the concrete walkway. He grasped the doorknob as he heard the soft squeak of a sole outside. "Be thankful this didn't turn out any worse than—"

Whenever he thought about it afterward, for the life of him Connor couldn't remember how the gun got into his hand. Even after racking his brains to reconstruct his actions, the nearest he would ever get to an answer was the dim recollection that his right hand had already been moving across his body as the door had opened.

They looked like agents. One of them was displaying an ID case with a photo and badge, and the other was reaching into an inner suit pocket, presumably to obtain his own identification.

"Agent Connor? I'm Agent Petrie and this is my partner, Agent Malden." The one holding out the ID case snapped it shut and gave a thin-lipped smile. "Area Director Jansen sent us to—"

Even as the logical part of Connor's mind was telling him the men confronting him had to be what they appeared to be and that he was about to make the worst mistake of his career, he made his move.

"Tess—get *down!*"

His shout cutting explosively across Petrie's words, Connor swung the gun he was holding around in a powerful arc toward the two agents.

Chapter Five

"Don't let Skinwalker get me, Tess!" Joey cried frantically.

Eyes still wide with shock at Connor's shouted warning, Tess whirled around to the bed, where her nephew was sitting bolt upright, his face drained of color. His gaze was dark with terror; he was staring at nothing.

He was having a nightmare. Relief flooded through her as she rushed to his side, but on its heels came quick fear.

"It's okay, Joey, I'm here."

Wrapping her arms around his shaking shoulders, she saw awareness returning to his eyes, and her own bewildered gaze darted back to the doorway in time to see the revolver in Connor's hand smash against the cheekbone of one of the agents standing in front of him. The air rushed from her lungs as completely as if she had taken the blow herself.

Virgil Connor had just attacked one of his own people. Either he'd suddenly lost his sanity, or...

...or he's working against the Agency. The terrifying possibility seemed the only explanation for

what she was witnessing, but it didn't make sense. If Connor had no intention of allowing her and Joey to reach Albuquerque, then why had he phoned Area Director Jansen? And why had—

She froze. Caught off guard, the man Connor had struck had staggered sideways and fallen to his knees outside the door. An object spun from his grasp and clattered to the ground.

The object was a gun. And Malden had been reaching for it *before* Connor had reacted.

"Under the bed!" Tess tightened her grip on her nephew's shoulders. "Get under the bed and stay there until I say it's safe to come out, understand, Joey? If something happens to me, do what Connor says."

Mutely he nodded. Any other nine-year-old would be firing questions at her, she thought, as he scrambled off the bed, but someone had made the monsters real for Joey.

Deep inside Tess a hot flame of rage ignited, flared dangerously high and then steadied into an icy fury. Whoever that person was, she told herself, she would make him pay for what he'd done....

If she and her newfound nephew got out of here alive.

In the few seconds it had taken to attend to Joey, the confrontation at the doorway had evolved with frightening speed. She took in the situation with a glance.

Petrie had obviously gone for his own weapon when his cohort, Malden, had fallen. It would have been simple for Connor to have thwarted the agent's intentions by opening fire, except for the possibility that a stray bullet from any ensuing gun battle might have found an innocent victim. As he had outside the diner, Connor had chosen not to take that risk. She saw worriedly that he'd dropped the revolver he'd used to disable Malden.

The man who'd identified himself as Agent Petrie had no such scruples. Even now he was attempting to bring the automatic in his grasp into position, but Connor, his height and weight definite advantages, was gaining the upper hand. Petrie's features contorted in agony, his right arm bent back at an angle, but still he didn't release his grip on his weapon.

"Drop the gun, or the next thing you hear'll be the sound of your arm breaking," Connor ground out. "I've heard that sound once or twice myself, and believe me, it takes the fight right out of a man."

The epithet Petrie grunted out in reply was made even more graphically obscene by the raw fury in his tone. Tess saw a flicker of distaste and reluctance cross Connor's face.

"If that's the way you want it," he said briefly. With no discernible effort, he forced the other man's arm back further, and from between Petrie's thin lips came a whistling noise.

"All...all right," he gasped. The fingers that had been clenched so tightly opened in defeat and the gun he'd been holding fell to the worn scrap of carpeting by the door. "Ease off, damn you!"

"Not until you tell me who sent you to kill Joey Begand," Connor said. She heard an edge of cold rage in his tone. "What happened to the real backup

Jansen was sending me? Did you and your partner ambush them along the way? And how did you intercept a secure communication between an area director's office and an agent in the field anyway, dammit?''

With every question he increased the pressure on Petrie's arm, and again a breath whistled painfully in the man's throat. Incredibly, this time it was accompanied by a rusty laugh.

''You're not even warm, Fed. Yeah, we were sent to eliminate the kid, and if we could we were supposed to make it look like you snapped and shot him yourself. But we didn't intercept—''

The first shot caught Connor high on the shoulder, breaking his hold on Petrie. Even as Tess's horrified glance took in Malden, still prone, but with his trouser leg pulled up to reveal an empty ankle holster, the man fired a second time. His wavering aim missed Connor and hit Petrie.

In the middle of Petrie's forehead a small, neat hole appeared. On the open door behind him was a brilliant explosion of scarlet. His eyes wide and sightless, slowly he collapsed to his knees, pitching face forward onto the carpet. Instant nausea rose in Tess.

But there was no time for squeamishness. Already Malden's unsteady aim was swinging back toward Connor. Forcing herself not to think about what she was doing, she threw herself across Petrie's lifeless body, her outstretched arm scrabbling past him for the automatic pistol he'd dropped only seconds ago.

Her fingers closed around it. Clumsily she flicked

the safety off, raised herself onto her elbows and
squeezed the trigger.

The report of her shot was overlaid with another,
louder discharge that came from behind and above
her. As if swatted by a giant hand, Malden lifted off
the ground, completing a half roll before landing
again, this time on his back. One knee jerked up and
then slid back down.

She'd just killed a man. This time when the bile
rose in her throat, Tess knew she wasn't going to be
able to keep it down. Scrambling to her feet, she took
a lurching step across Petrie's body toward the door,
her gaze fixed on the tired clump of bushes just beyond the walkway.

"No!"

Connor's arm shot out as she stumbled by him.
Almost losing her balance, she struck blindly out at
him.

"Let me by, Connor. I'm going to be—"

Five years ago she'd gone backpacking in the Sangre de Cristo Mountains, Tess recalled. It had been in
the weeks following the Joy Gaynor incident—which
was why, on her third morning out, she'd found herself standing on a ledge a hundred feet above a valley
staring into the charcoal predawn and waiting for the
sun to show itself over the horizon before doing what
she'd decided to do.

The sun hadn't shown itself. Instead the heavens
overhead had split open with a crash so loud that
she'd clapped her hands to her ears in pain and had
nearly fallen from the ledge.

But she hadn't fallen, and the dozens of lightning

strikes that had lit up the mountains over the next hours hadn't touched her. It had been as if some Great Being had chosen that way to show her that her time to die wasn't upon her yet, no matter what she'd intended.

When the storm had passed, she'd hiked out of the mountains, had driven back to Albuquerque and had handed in her resignation at work—just a formality, since she'd known she no longer had a future with any legitimate newspaper. Within days she'd landed her job at the *Eye-Opener,* and although she'd known she couldn't put the past completely behind her, gradually she'd learned not to dwell on it.

But she'd never forgotten how that first crack of lightning in the Sangre de Cristos had sounded, Tess thought now—as if the very mountains themselves were being split asunder. So, as Connor jerked her backward, her first thought was for Joey, still hiding under the metal bedstead and a prime target for any bolt of lightning following the one that had just lit up the night in front of the motel unit, so close to Connor's parked sedan that it actually seemed to have come from the car.

Her second thought was the realization that what she'd just seen wasn't lightning at all, but an explos—

"Take cover! The gas tank's going to blow next!"

Before she could react to Connor's hoarse command, a deafening *whump!* came from the vicinity of the sedan. Tess had a glimpse of the car lifting off the pavement before a towering fireball of yellow flames hid it from view.

"Dammit, woman—*down!*"

One strong arm snugging her tightly to his body, his other hand spread protectively wide against the back of her head, Connor pulled her to him. She felt herself flying through the air, his arms around her.

They hit the motel room floor heavily a heartbeat later, Connor on the bottom and taking the brunt of the fall. In one swift movement he hooked an ankle around the nearest leg of the dresser, yanking it in front of them, but not before Tess felt a stinging sensation in the back of her thigh.

Against the front of the dresser she heard several fast thuds, as if tennis balls were being volleyed at it. Across the room the telephone jingled once and smashed to the floor. With a high, icy sound of glass shattering, pieces of the dresser's mirror flashed around them, while sheered-off metal from the explosion outside turned into flying shrapnel.

The bed was in the safest area of the room, shielded by the half-open door of the unit from the storm of debris. Thank God she'd told Joey to hide under there.

From the parking lot outside came a metallic groaning noise that ended with a jarring crash. The abrupt silence that followed was broken only by the roar of flames.

"The car just collapsed onto its axles," Connor muttered from somewhere near her ear. "You okay?"

He was still holding her, but as he spoke he loosened his grip and peered intently into her face. Tess nodded.

"I…I'm okay." She heard the tremor in her voice and changed her nod to a shake of her head. "No,

I'm not okay. How could I be? I...I *killed* a man, Connor. He was going to kill us and I didn't have any choice, but I took a life. I killed a man.''

"You killed my car. I killed Malden," Connor said abstractedly. He began to get to his feet. "We've got to get Joey out of here before the police arrive and decide to engage in a jurisdictional pissing contest with me. I'd win, but I don't want to waste time getting into it with—''

He paused, his glance sharpening on her. Swiftly he sank back down beside her and took both her hands in his. "I killed him, Tess. I fired just before you did, and my bullet caught him in the upper chest. Your bullet was lower, which was why it ricocheted off the pavement into the car's gas tank.''

The apparent lack of emotion in his voice was belied by his tight grip on her fingers. Virgil Connor wasn't the man she'd first seen him as, Tess thought slowly, her gaze locked on his. She had the sudden certainty that he wasn't even the man he saw himself as. He'd glimpsed her horror at the belief that she'd been responsible for taking Malden down, and some part of him had needed to take that horror away from her.

He got to his feet, pulling her up with him. She saw the spasm of pain that crossed his features, and realized with a start that a similar spasm had involuntarily crossed hers.

"You're hurt." His brows drew together. "Where?"

"My leg twinges, that's all. I think I pulled a muscle when we landed on the floor." He was all business again, she noted. She followed his lead. "Forget me, what about you?"

As she spoke she remembered what had happened just prior to Malden's death. She bit back a gasp.

"You were shot, weren't you?" Placing one palm on his chest, she began to draw aside the right lapel of his jacket. His hand clamped around her wrist, but too late to stop her.

Beneath the suit fabric one whole side of the formerly white shirt was drenched in blood. This time her gasp was audible.

"We've got to get you to a doctor," she said decisively. Releasing his lapel and shaking off his hand, she stepped out from behind the dresser. "Joey!" Ignoring the state of the room, she sped over to the relatively untouched area near the bed and knelt beside it. "Joey, it's safe to come out now. Are you all right?"

"I think so." Amazingly, as the nine-year-old scooted out on his back from under the bed like a mechanic from under a car, his eyes shone with excitement. "Wow, that was something, huh? What happened—did they use a rocket launcher or—"

His mouth dropped open as he surveyed the room. "Holy sh—"

"They didn't use a rocket launcher," Tess interjected quickly. "And Joey, listen to me—both of those men who came to hurt us are dead. One of them doesn't—" She took his hands. "One of them doesn't look so good, so when we walk out I want you to keep your eyes on me, okay? This isn't like in the movies, and I don't want you to see it."

Partly visible, hunkered down on the other side of the door, Connor was covering Petrie with a blanket. But she didn't want to take the chance of Joey catching sight of anything that might fuel his already-disturbing nightmares.

"Okay, Tess." Joey swallowed. He squared his shoulders, his gaze still on hers. "I won't look, but I'm not sorry they're dead. They came here to kill me, didn't they? They prob'ly didn't figure on running into you."

Connor had been right, Tess thought helplessly. She should have nipped Joey's hero-worship of her in the bud two days ago, but now wasn't the time to set him straight. She stood.

From somewhere farther down the row of units came raised voices, the first she'd heard since Connor had opened the door to Malden and Petrie. Obviously, some of the motel's guests were gathering the courage to investigate.

"I guess they didn't," she said weakly. "But Connor was the one who mostly fought them off, and he got hurt. We're going to have to take him to a hospital right away."

"No, we're not." Connor strode toward them. "For all we know those two weren't working alone. We're going to put some distance between us and this place, and then I'm going to contact Jansen again and arrange a secure meet."

Before she could protest, he went on, his tone impatient. "It's not your call, Tess. Come on, let's go."

The body by the door was just a shape beneath the blanket Connor had thrown over it, and although Malden still lay outside on the walkway, mercifully his prone figure was obscured by shadows. Still, as she hurried Joey by, Tess found herself envying Connor's seeming unconcern.

He was Belacana, non-Navajo, she reminded herself. To him a dead body was just a dead body. Even if he understood what an Enemy Way was, the concept of a warrior undergoing a ceremony to rid himself of the ghosts of those he'd killed wouldn't fit his logical view of the world.

She didn't know how much credence she put in the old beliefs herself, she thought unhappily as they headed across the parking lot. All she knew was that she wished she had some—

"I got corn pollen," Joey said beside her in a small voice. His backpack slung over his shoulder, he fumbled under the grimy neckband of his tee. "I think you're supposed to sprinkle some on your tongue and your head. That's what Mac told me when he gave it to me, anyway."

"Mac? John MacLeish?"

Connor was ahead of them, but from the stiffening of his posture as she spoke, Tess knew he'd heard her reference to the man the FBI was hunting. *Too bad, Agent,* she thought with a spurt of defiance. *If you think I'm going to take this opportunity to see if Joey's memory's starting to come back, you're wrong. Right now us two Dineh have more important business to attend to.*

"Yeah. He said the worst thing that could happen to a man was if he forgot who he was and where he came from. He told me I should be proud to be one of the People." Joey glanced up. "Some kids had been ragging me, calling me a dumb Indian."

"I see."

She did see, Tess thought. The hardscrabble environment of the streets was a perfect breeding ground for ignorance and racism; although also, from what she understood Joey to be saying, equally a place where a homeless man's rough kindness could reveal itself in giving the gift of pride to a child. For the first time she found herself wondering what kind of person the mysterious MacLeish was. A killer, yes, judging from the Agency's case against him. But he'd seemingly behaved with compassion and sensitivity toward the boy.

And now he was supposed to be looking for Joey to kill him. She frowned.

"There's enough here for all of us," Joey continued. "Mac said pollen's a reminder of the Way, so using it keeps the ghosts back. You...you want some, too, Connor?"

They'd reached the other side of the parking area and the lone vehicle sitting there. As Tess cast an glance back at the motel, a man and a woman hurriedly exited a unit, the male still zipping his trousers and the woman buttoning her blouse. The two of them got into a car and sped away.

Most of the motel's clientele would have the same aversion to coming forward as witnesses, she thought. That explained why no one had tried to stop Connor and Joey and her from leaving a scene that included a burning car and two bodies.

"Want some what? Oh." Connor shook his head

as Joey held out the small washed-leather pouch that hung on a rawhide thong around his neck. "Pollen, right? No, don't waste it on me, Joey. But you go ahead and use it while I unlock the car."

Tess stared at Connor as he withdrew a key tag with a single key on it from his jacket pocket. Joey nudged her, and she switched her attention back to him as he tapped out a scattering of pollen grains into her palm and then his own. Slipping the thong-tied bag under his T-shirt again, with a child's solemnity he put a pinch of the substance onto his outstretched tongue and uncertainly dusted what was left over his head. He looked at her expectantly. Feeling slightly foolish—she'd been raised with so little knowledge of her own heritage that for all she knew they were doing this all wrong, she told herself in mild embarrassment—she copied his actions.

The pollen tasted nutty and not unpleasant. *Like corn meal,* she thought, *but silkier and more golden.* As she sprinkled the rest of the grains on her hair her embarrassment faded.

Right here and right now the Navajo Nation had a population of two, she realized slowly—Joey Begand and Tess Smith. They were on the run, but it wasn't the first time the People had been forced to flee. They had only a sketchy idea of the ways of their culture. But in the not-so-distant past that same disjointed separation from the Way had been harshly imposed on succeeding generations of Navajo, and yet the Way had endured.

Beauty behind me, Beauty in front of me, Beauty above me, Beauty all—

"Beauty all around me."

Joey's young voice finished the last line of the chant, and only then did Tess realize she'd spoken the words out loud. She met his gaze.

Five minutes ago she'd felt sick—sick to her soul, sickened by the violence she'd witnessed and the knowledge that there were men in the world evil enough to take the life of a child. As she and Joey had hurried out of the motel room she'd felt as if that foglike evil was reaching out for them.

She didn't feel like that anymore. Neither did Joey, she could tell. The hectic excitement he'd displayed was no longer in evidence; instead, his eyes were calm and trusting.

She didn't know if she believed in ghosts, Tess thought, and she wasn't certain she believed corn pollen had any special significance. But if she did, she would say that the pollen in the little leather bag John MacLeish had given Joey had been a protection against the lingering spirits of two killers.

"Get in. Joey, you bunk down in the back seat and see if you can get some shut-eye."

Beside them, Connor had unlocked the sedan and was waiting by the open door of the vehicle. Suddenly comprehending his plan, she darted a glance at Joey.

The fear was back in his gaze as he stared at the sedan. He made no move to get in.

"We…we can't take this car," Tess muttered. "This is Petrie and Malden's car, right? We can't take it."

He wouldn't understand, she thought. She wasn't

sure she did, either, but she couldn't argue with her feelings. The sick dread was back, stronger than ever.

While Connor had been covering Malden's body, he'd obviously removed the vehicle's keys from the dead man's pocket. She could see how a Belacana might view that as an expedient solution to their transportation problem, but even if she set aside her own aversion to entering the sedan, it was plain Joey wasn't going to be able to.

"What do you mean, we can't take this car?" Connor looked from her to Joey and back at her again. "It's the only one available to us. You blew mine up, remember?"

"It's *their* car," Joey said thinly. His voice shook. "If we take it, their *chindi* will come after us, and not even the pollen'll be strong enough to keep them away."

"For God's—" Connor exhaled and turned a frustrated glare on Tess. "You want to tell me what the hell he's talking about? What's a *chindi?*"

"A ghost. You can't use a dead man's possessions or his ghost will follow you," she said rapidly. "On the Dinetah you'll sometimes see an abandoned hogan, and except for the fact that it has a hole knocked into the north wall it looks like a perfectly serviceable home. That's a death hogan. Someone died in there before the family could take him outside to die, and when that happens the hogan is never used again by anyone. The family knocks a hole into the north wall to signify that a *chindi* was released inside."

"Okay, but this isn't a hogan," a muscle moved in his jaw, "and we don't have a choice here."

"I'm not getting in." Joey's bottom lip stuck out stubbornly, and for a moment he looked like a smaller version of the man he was confronting. "There's nothing we can do to stop them from following us if we take their car."

His words struck a chord of memory in Tess. She'd heard something once, hadn't she? Something about how to confuse a vengeful *chindi* enough to stop it from—

"Wait here," she said swiftly.

She caught a glimpse of Connor's thunderous expression as she ran back to the motel. It was no less thunderous when she returned a couple of minutes later, but she ignored him.

"Get in the car, Joey." She mustered a crooked smile. "Go on, it's okay now. I fixed it so they can't follow."

"How'd you fix—"

Joey's disbelieving question was interrupted by a ringing noise. Connor's frown deepened, and from an inner pocket of his jacket he retrieved a cell phone. He squinted at the display.

"It's my partner, Paula." For the first time since she'd met him, Tess saw a real smile lift the corners of his mouth. "Paula Geddes," he elaborated. "She was on duty the night the safe house was blown and Bill Danzig was killed. If she's calling, she must have been released from hospital."

He'd mentioned Geddes in passing earlier, but not that the female agent was his partner. As well as his concern for his kidnapped witness, he'd had the strain of worrying about the woman he worked alongside to contend with, Tess thought as he turned away to take the call. Maybe that added strain had been the final straw that had momentarily weakened his self-control when he'd kissed her.

Whether it had been or not, she knew instinctively that Virgil Connor wouldn't accept it as an excuse for what he'd done. She could understand that, because she hadn't been able to excuse herself for her reaction to—

"Get in the car, Joey. If I have to, I'll pick you up and put you in, but we're getting out of here now. You, too, Tess."

Connor's tone was sharp. Tossing the cell phone on the dashboard, he slid in behind the wheel and started the car.

"Do what he says," Tess reassured the still-hesitant child, feeling far from reassured herself. "I'll explain later, but it's okay now."

She waited until Joey was in the back seat and buckling his seat belt before getting in herself. Even before she closed the passenger-side door Connor hit the gas.

"Change of plans," he said tightly. "We're not heading for Albuquerque, and I'm not going to be setting up a meet with Area Director Jansen."

His face was etched with tension. "Paula checked herself out of hospital half an hour ago. She said she wanted to warn me as soon as possible."

"Warn you about what?"

"About Arne Jansen." His reply was toneless. "Paula's got proof he arranged the attack on the safe house."

"He's working against the Agency?" Tess gasped. "But…but why?"

Connor shook his head. "I don't know. But I do know one thing."

His fingers tightened on the steering wheel, and he glanced at her, his gaze bleak. "If Paula's right and he's a traitor, then Jansen deliberately sent Petrie and Malden to kill us at that motel tonight."

Chapter Six

According to the Navajo origin myth there had been three, some said four, worlds before this one. Tess caught herself yawning and forced herself to concentrate on the latest subject she'd chosen to occupy her mind. But maybe the Dineh explanation of how the universe began wasn't the best choice, she admitted. The first of those worlds had been one of unending darkness, and right now it seemed as though she'd been driving through that first world for the past five hours.

Joey was fast asleep in the back seat. Beside her Connor stirred restlessly, and she darted a worried glance at him.

When his increasingly erratic steering had nearly landed them in an irrigation ditch near Socorro he'd wordlessly pulled over. She'd seen the physical effort it had cost him just to walk around to the passenger side of the car, and she'd considered discarding the plan he'd earlier outlined and driving him straight to the nearest hospital.

Even as the thought had gone through her mind his

hand had clamped around her wrist with surprising strength.

"Promise me you'll get us to the Double B," he'd said hoarsely. "Hawkins'll know what to do for me, and Joey and you'll be safe there. By now Jansen will have every hospital emergency room in the state under surveillance."

She'd tried one last time to dissuade him. "But a ranch, Connor? That's what the Double B is, and your Del Hawkins is just a rancher. How can you be so sure we'll be safe there?"

"Because the Double B's where you go when you've come to the end of the line, honey." His tone had been so slurred she'd known he wasn't aware he'd used an endearment. "And Del's not just a rancher, he's a lifesaver. He saved mine once, a long time ago. Promise me you'll get us there."

"All right, I promise. But after what I explained to you about *chindis* at the motel, I hope you realize that if you look like you're about to draw your last breath, I'm leaving you by the roadside, Agent Connor," she'd replied, hoping her tartness masked her worry over his condition. "If you're so determined to get to the Double B, then don't you dare die on me."

She hadn't been sure he was still tracking well enough to respond, but incredibly, as he released her wrist he gave her a faint grin. "I never did ask you," he'd murmured, his lashes drifting down to his cheekbones. "How did you convince Joey it was okay to get into the car?"

"I switched Malden's shoes," she'd replied briefly. "I put his left shoe on his right foot, and the right on his left. That's supposed to confuse ghosts when they try to follow you. It was enough to reassure Joey, anyway.''

Instead of the laughter she'd half expected, Connor had remained silent for a moment. When she'd glanced at him she'd seen his eyes were open again.

''That took guts, lady,'' he'd said softly. ''You told me you weren't brought up in the Way, but it still went against everything you believed in to touch a dead body, didn't it?''

''I'm not the first Dineh to have to get over it. I've heard many Navajo medical students dread their first anatomy class, knowing they'll have to work on a cadaver, but they grit their teeth and do it.'' She'd frowned. ''But no, it wasn't pleasant. And I noticed something odd.''

''The bastard was dressed like the complete FBI agent, except he was wearing running shoes?'' Connor's tone had hardened. ''His carelessness probably saved our lives. I knew something wasn't right even as I opened the door to them, and later I realized I must have picked up on the squeak of runners, instead of the sound of a regulation sole. If I hadn't, I'll bet his buddy Petrie would have taken me out while Malden was handing over his phony photo and badge.''

The slur had been back in his speech, and minutes later Tess had realized he'd either fallen asleep or had lapsed into unconsciousness. The former, she hoped, risking another desperate glance at him before switching her attention back to the deserted road in front of her. Because if it was the latter, she wasn't sure she was going to get Virgil Connor to the Double B Ranch in time.

The Double B's where you go when you've come to the end of the line... She had no idea what he'd meant by that. But if Del Hawkins was the lifesaver Connor seemed to think he was and if the Double B really was as much of a last-resort refuge as he'd said, she was willing to give it a shot.

"Because we really *are* at the end of the line," she muttered to herself. "Connor said it himself—except for Paula, he can't trust anyone in the Agency at this point. Until he figures out what Jansen's game is, everyone's suspect."

And there was another reason why Connor couldn't simply walk into the nearest police station to present his side of the story. That reason had been what had prompted Paula's urgent call to the partner she trusted so implicitly.

"An emergency alert went out sometime tonight to every operative involved in the search for Joey," Connor had said in an undertone as they'd sped away from the motel. "When Paula overheard some agents who'd stopped to see her at the hospital, she checked herself out against her doctor's protests and phoned me right away." He'd flicked a glance at Tess. "We've been partners since I was transferred to New Mexico a year and a half ago, and we've been in some pretty tight situations together. She said even if the head of the Bureau himself told her I'd turned traitor, she wouldn't believe it."

"Traitor?" Tess's voice had risen in shock, and

hastily she'd lowered it, not wanting Joey to hear. "Like Rick Leroy?"

He'd nodded tightly. "Jansen's saying he has reason to suspect I was involved with Leroy in what happened at the safe house. I'm to be considered armed and dangerous, and to be taken out by any means possible."

As he likely would have been if his call to Jansen from the motel hadn't prompted the area director to send a couple of outside killers to eliminate him, rather than take the chance that a pair of legitimate agents would attempt to bring Connor in without bloodshed, Tess thought now, slowing as her headlights illuminated a particularly rough stretch of road ahead. But why *had* Connor suddenly become a liability to his director—such a liability that the man had as much as put out a shoot-on-sight order on him, and had bolstered that action by contacting Petrie and Malden?

The alert had been issued hours before Connor had contacted Arne Jansen with the news that he'd found Joey, so the fact that the Agency's young witness was being brought in couldn't have been what had panicked the man. Or could it?

"It's the only explanation," she muttered, her pulse quickening. "Jansen knew Connor had Joey *before* Connor phoned him. He knew because the busboy must have reported seeing a woman forcing a federal agent into a car at gunpoint."

And when Jansen had learned the Agency's missing witness was in Connor's custody, he hadn't seen that as good news.

''He must be afraid Joey's memory's come back. From the start that's what this was all about. As far as Jansen's concerned, Joey's a ticking time bomb that could explode at any minute.''

Tess switched on the dashboard maplight and glanced at the scrap of paper on which Connor had written the directions to the Double B. The turnoff to the ranch would be coming up soon, she saw. She switched off the map light, but not before her apprehensive gaze had taken in the sheen of sweat on Connor's brow and the blotchy pallor under his tan.

A ball of ice settled itself in the pit of her stomach. He was dying, she thought with numb certainty. It was no longer a matter of whether she could get him to his destination, because even if she did, this time the Double B and Del Hawkins wouldn't be able to save his life. He'd lost so much blood that one side of his suit jacket was a dark red black. He needed to be on a gurney being raced at top speed into an operating room right now.

Pain lanced through her, so sharply thất it seemed a blade had flashed through the darkness and unerringly found her soul.

He was going to die, and he'd never lived—or if he had, it had been so long ago that he probably couldn't remember what it felt like. She'd known just by looking at him that he kept a box around himself and his emotions, and that somewhere inside that box was the real Virgil Connor. She'd known because she'd caught a glimpse of the real man when he'd kissed—

A massive gray form suddenly loomed up out of

the darkness into the headlights. Even as she slammed her foot down as hard as she could on the brake, Tess heard the left rear tire blow.

The back end of the car slewed violently to the right, as if a gigantic grappling hook had suddenly yanked it sideways. Through the windshield the headlights cut a swath of illumination that swung dizzily to the left, and for a moment she saw the baked earth of the downward-sloping embankment that paralleled the road thrown into brilliant relief. The left front tire began to slip on the gravelled edge of the small drop.

Frantically Tess turned the steering wheel to the right in a desperate attempt to pull the car out of its counter-clockwise spin. She felt the three remaining tires slip, felt them grab, and then the nightmarish view in front of the windshield began swinging the other way.

Before the second spin jolted the wheel from her hands, she realized she'd overcorrected. The world became a swift blur.

"Tess!"

"Hold on, Joey! We're going to—"

Halfway through its circular spinout and while the car was actually traveling backward, its ruined tire slipped over the edge of the roadway. Tipped backward in her seat, Tess saw the beams of the headlights shoot crazily up into the night sky and felt a slamming jolt against her hips as the sedan, its engine stalling out, came to an abrupt halt in the shallow drop.

For a second she couldn't move. Through the partially open driver's side window she heard one last spill of dirt rattle against the side of the car and then everything was silent.

"Holy cow, what *happened?*"

Joey's question broke through her temporary paralysis and she twisted around in her seat, ignoring the hot pain that shot through the back of her thigh. He looked none the worse for wear, his expression more startled than fearful. Fierce thankfulness rushed through her.

"We had an accident, Joey. One of the tires blew and I couldn't keep the car on the road." Her gaze swept over his seat-belted figure. "Did you hit your head or anything?"

"Nah." He swiped the ever-present strand of black hair out of his eyes. "I was asleep and the next thing I knew we were going in a circle. How come the air bags didn't go off?"

"Because they're made to deploy in a frontal collision, not when you slide butt-end off the road," she said distractedly. "Joey, flick on the dome light. I...I need to check on Connor."

He did as she asked. Unlatching her own seat belt, Tess bent over the unmoving man strapped into the passenger seat.

He was dead. His face was the color of wax, and the lips that earlier this evening had been so hot and urgent on hers were slightly parted. No breath came from between them.

She'd only known Virgil Connor for the space of a few hours, and for most of that time they'd been on opposite sides of an unscalably high fence. Even when they'd kissed there had been an electric antagonism between them. But for a while they'd been fighting on the same side.

She would remember two things about him. One would be his stubborn sense of duty. The other would be those beautiful, crystal-gray eyes that had looked on her with anger, with exasperation and, for one brief moment, with raw desire.

When the pain slammed into her it seemed to catch her just under her heart, with such unexpectedness that it drove a choking gasp from her. Connor's left hand was hanging down by the side of his seat, and for no sane reason at all Tess grasped it between her two palms, bringing it to her cheek.

"Is Connor dead?"

There was none of the fear in Joey's voice that he'd displayed back at the motel, but only a wrenching sadness that seemed far too adult an emotion for his nine years. Still pressing Connor's hand to her cheek, Tess gave a single nod.

"He…he lost a lot of blood, Joey," she whispered, barely able to get the words out. "I should have gotten him to a hospital instead of—"

Beneath her fingertips she felt something. She froze, the rest of her answer dying in her throat.

She felt it again—the barest flicker of a lethargic pulse in the broad-boned wrist she was holding. Wild hope flared in her and almost immediately was quenched.

They were in the middle of nowhere, in a smashed-up car. And although Connor was still miraculously alive, unless another miracle came along right this very instant, his death had merely been delayed.

"Back the truck up, Del, and give me some light here! I think there's someone in this car!"

The shouted request came from the road. Jerking her head up, Tess saw the powerful beams of a set of headlights turning her way. Instinctively she threw her arm up to shield her eyes from the dazzling glare.

The next moment she was fumbling at the door. "Joey, stay here," she babbled. "I don't want you trying to get out of this car until we see how stable it is. I'll be right back."

The door opened halfway and jammed on an outcrop of rock, but halfway was enough. Tess started to scramble up the bank, fell to her knees and pushed herself upright again just as a strong hand wrapped itself around her arm to steady her.

"Del?" she gasped. She clutched at the man, taking in the streaks of silver in the dark hair, the weatherbeaten tan of his face. "Are you Del Hawkins?"

"No, ma'am, my name's Dan'l Bird." There was a soft drawl, more southern than western, to his speech, but his gaze was sharp. "Looks as if you had yourself a little accident, ma'am. Anyone else in the car?"

"What's going on, Daniel? Anybody hurt?"

A second man, portlier and shorter than the first, trotted toward them from the direction of the heavy-duty pickup idling at the other side of the road. Even as Tess gazed wildly at the vehicle, she saw a third figure alight stiffly from the cab on the driver's side. As he started across the road she saw the interlocked *B* letters on the truck door.

"This lady's shooken up pretty bad, Doc," Bird

said in his soft voice. "How be you wait here with her and I'll take a look-see in case there's someone in there I can help?"

"There's a child in the back seat." Tess tried to control the unsteadiness in her tone. "He wasn't injured. But the man who was with me in the front is badly wounded."

She saw the quick frown that appeared on the face of the portly man at her choice of words. She went on, her voice a rasp. "Not when the car went off the road. He's been shot. I…I think he's dying."

Bird was already making his way down the embankment to the sedan. His friend sucked in a breath, and brows that held a touch of what must once have been fiery red drew together.

"Where was he hit? Is the bullet still in him?"

Like Bird, he was wearing jeans and a denim shirt, but on him they didn't look as if they were his normal attire. Coupled with his brisk reaction and the questions he was firing at her, Tess belatedly remembered how Bird had addressed him.

"You're a doctor?"

"Surgeon. Or I was," he corrected himself. "Retired now. Don't worry, we'll get your friend to a hospital in time. I'll ride beside him in the truck and monitor—"

"He's not going to make it," she broke in. "Don't you understand? He's at the end of the line. That's why he wouldn't let me take him to a hospital in the first place—because he needed to get to the Double B and Del Hawkins."

Fresh hopelessness overwhelmed her. The man in

front of her meant well, she told herself. This situation wasn't his fault; it was hers. She never should have kept her word to Connor, never should have delayed getting him proper medical help, no matter what the possible consequences.

A rancher and a ranch. Connor had seen them as a refuge and a lifesaver. Judging from the sign on the truck, they were on or close to Double B land, and through a process of elimination the lean man with the oddly stiff gait who'd just joined them had to be Hawkins, since she'd heard Bird call out Del's name.

According to what Connor had believed, now was when everything would start going right, Tess thought in bitter self-recrimination.

"Fella with a gunshot wound in that car, Del," the doctor said tersely. "The lady says he's in critical condition, won't make it to a hospital in time, but we're going to have to try. I'll lend Daniel a hand in getting him into the truck."

"We need something we can use as a stretcher. There you go, son." Bird hoisted Joey over the lip of the embankment. As he set the boy on his feet, the face he turned to his two companions was somber. "You're the sawbones, Scotty, but I'd say the lady's right. I don't rightly see her man's got much of a chance—not less'n he gets topped up with a few pints of blood within the next half hour."

"First things first." Hawkins's tone was no sharper than Bird's had been, but as soon as he spoke it was indefinably obvious that he had taken command. He went on. "Daniel, there's a tarp in the bed of the truck. We'll rig a field stretcher out of it. Van, see if you can do something to stabilize your patient for the journey.''

He met the doctor's swiftly dubious glance. A corner of his mouth lifted briefly. ''I know the legendary Dr. Van Zane has spent the past thirty years waltzing into operating theaters, performing his miracles, and walzing out again while teams of doctors and nurses and assistants took care of the tedious details. But hell, Van, I seem to recall a redheaded medic in 'Nam who could tie a tourniquet with his teeth, cut through a man's blood-filled boot, and prepare an injection all while humming a Jimmi Hendrix tune under his breath.''

Van Zane held his gaze. ''I still like Hendrix. The music was the only thing I cared to remember about those days…the music and the friends I made, which is why one of the first things on my post-retirement list of things to do was to make this trip out west and catch up with a couple of old buddies. I'll do my best, Del.''

With less grace and more effort than Daniel Bird had displayed, he made his way down the bank to the sedan. In a moment Bird, a tarpaulin bundled under one arm, joined him.

''Why don't you take your son to the truck?'' Hawkins had been watching his friends' efforts to extract Connor from the sedan, but now he turned to her. ''As soon as Van and Daniel get your husband settled in the pickup's cargo bed, we'll be on our way.'' He frowned. ''The hospital in Gallup's out of the question, if your husband's condition is as serious as you say. But there's a clinic in Last Chance. That's only fifty minutes' drive from—"

"He said you were a lifesaver." Tess's voice trembled. "All I see is a man giving orders and not lifting a finger himself. Why aren't you helping your friends bring him up?"

Feeling Joey press closer to her, she put an arm around him and with her other hand she dashed the sudden moisture from her eyes. "He's not my husband. I've only known him for a few hours. But even those few hours were enough to convince me he deserved better from a man he seemed to think was his friend."

"A friend?" Hawkins looked confused. "Do I know—"

He'd taken a step toward her. The gravel shifted slightly under his foot, and the next moment he lurched forward, only his quick grab at her shoulder saving him from falling. He released her with a swift apology and steadied himself.

Shame burned through Tess. She knew what he was going to tell her before he spoke.

"My days of scrambling up hills ended in Vietnam, I'm afraid," he said hoarsely. "These—" he rapped his knuckles on a jeans-clad thigh, which gave off a hollow sound "—these aren't the legs the good Lord issued me. They get me around, but on a surface like this I really should use a cane."

"I'm sorry. Virg—" She bit her lip. "Connor didn't tell me that part."

"*Connor?*" In the harsh illumination from the

truck's headlights Hawkins's features froze. "Virgil Connor?"

"Steady, now, steady. Haul yourself up there, Doc."

The corners of the tarp had been lashed to long two-by-fours. Beside Del, Bird lowered the lengths of wood he was holding almost to the ground as with a grunt Van Zane hoisted his end over the lip of the rise and set it down. The doctor began to clamber up the bank unimpeded.

"He's still alive, but just barely," Bird said in a low tone. "Ma'am, your boy don't need to see his daddy like this. You get along to the pickup and we'll take care of your man."

"He's not her husband," Del informed him tightly. "He's Virgil Connor. He used to be one of my boys. He was trying to get back to the ranch, apparently."

His tone was harsh. Wrenching her gaze from Connor's still features, Tess saw the older man's jaw work soundlessly, saw the sudden gleam of anguish in his eyes. Van Zane picked up his ends of the makeshift stretcher.

"Connor's not going to live long enough to get him to the clinic at Last Chance, Van." Del lifted his gaze to the doctor's frowning face. "We're taking him home. We're taking him to the Double B."

"But the man needs—"

"The man needs blood, I know." Hawkins's voice was a whiplash. "And he's going to get it—in a person-to-person transfusion in the kitchen of the Double B. Don't tell me it's impossible, Van, because I've seen you do it in the field."

He smiled tightly. "Hear me and hear me good, old buddy. Even if I have to stand over you with my service revolver while you operate, Virgil Connor's going to live. You're going to pull him through, dammit—and that's an order."

Chapter Seven

"Your ex-Double B bad boy is damned lucky his blood group's Type AB, which makes him what we call a universal recipient," Van Zane grunted four hours later in the ranch's kitchen. "Luckier still that you remembered that from the year he spent here. He's going to make it, so if you've got that service revolver close at hand, Hawkins, you can lock it up again."

From her position on an old-fashioned daybed a few feet away, Tess had been alternating between nibbles of cookie and sips from the mug of tea Del had given her. When he'd offered the refreshment twenty minutes earlier she'd declined, wanting only to close her eyes and pull the daybed's crocheted throw up to her chin, but he hadn't taken no for an answer.

"Doctor's orders," he'd instructed her. "As Daniel put it, you're not much bigger'n half a minute, and you donated more than your share of what's now pumping through Virgil's veins. Tea and cookies and rest is prescribed. How's your—"

He'd stopped abruptly. A hint of color had risen under the weatherbeaten tan of his face.

"How's my butt?" Tess had supplied, past the point of shyness. "It feels better than it did with an inch of steel splinter in it. That must have happened during the explosion."

She'd seen Del's blank look. "Of Connor's car," she'd supplied. "That was after those two phony agents tried to kill him. It's all tied up with Joey and why we couldn't go to a hospital and the fact that no one can know we're here, Del."

"No one's going to know," he'd assured her. "Daniel's back at the scene of the accident right now towing the car so no local deputy sees it and runs a check on the plates. I want to hear the whole story, but it can wait. You lie there and take it easy, sweetheart."

He'd squeezed her hand with the same gentleness he'd shown Joey when the nine-year-old had refused to be taken to one of the upstairs bedrooms and had insisted on bedding down on the living room couch. Tess knew the young boy's desire to stay close was based on his fear of the monsters he dreamed about.

Two real monsters had come terrifyingly close to taking Connor's life tonight, she thought now as the screen door that led from the kitchen to the verandah opened and Daniel Bird entered. Answering Del's glance of inquiry with a quick thumbs-up sign, Bird joined his friends at the massive pine table. As Del and Van Zale brought Daniel up to speed on Connor's status, Tess noted the easy interaction between them.

If not for Del's decisive actions, Daniel's help and Van Zane's expertise, Connor would have died. As soon as they'd reached the ranch, Van and Daniel had transported Connor to the house. Joey had accompanied Del to a supply room attached to the nearby horse barn—Tess had gathered that Appaloosas were raised on the property—and she herself had been ordered by Van Zane to spread blankets on the floor next to the kitchen table.

"Good light, plenty of room and running water," the retired surgeon had muttered as he and Daniel transferred an unconscious Connor to the thick pile of blankets. "I've seen worse operating conditions. Hop up on the table, sweet-pea."

Just as he and Del had addressed Joey as "champ" and "tiger" and each other as "buddy," they'd seemed equally at ease tossing casual endearments her way. Tess had hesitated.

"I don't mind taking the floor," she'd protested. "Surely it's better for Connor to have the table?"

Van Zane had been in the process of cutting through Connor's suit jacket with a pair of scissors. He'd completed his task before glancing at her.

"Now's as good a time as any to explain to you how the procedure's going to work," he said, not unkindly. "Since this is a pretty primitive setup for a transfusion, I'm going to be relying on gravity to get your blood into this big fella. I'll be taking it from your brachial artery—that's the one at the front of your arm—and letting it flow into one of his veins," he'd added. "Arteries pump with a stronger pressure. We don't want the blood flowing the wrong way."

He'd pursed his lips. "It's not going to be a big ball of fun for you," he'd admitted gruffly. "But you're our best shot. Del's out of the question. So am

I, naturally. Daniel had a couple of beer at dinner after the rodeo we attended, and unless Connor needs more blood than you can spare, I'd rather not take the chance of using his tonight. Maybe in a few hours, if I have to.''

Joey had burst in at that point, obviously sent ahead by the slower-moving Del. With a smile and a word of praise, Van Zane had taken some supplies from him.

''Were these used on *horses?*'' Joey had asked, his tone a mixture of mild disapproval and keen interest.

The surgeon had grinned, and Tess had mustered a smile. ''They're for horses,'' she'd informed him. ''Foals, actually, which is why they're not too big to use on people. But they're all in sealed packages, see? Del said he keeps transfusion lines and sutures and needles in case of emergencies when he can't get the vet out in time.''

Del had entered the room then, and with a nod at Van Zane, Daniel had lured Joey out of the kitchen with a casual reference to a litter of puppies residing in a box on the verandah. Tess had lain back on the table, suddenly nervous, and she'd felt Del's hand wrapping around her own.

''Virgil still have an attitude problem?'' he'd said, his eyes on hers. Tess had felt the coolness of an alcohol swab, and then Van Zane's deft fingers holding her upper arm. As if to take both her mind and his off what was happening, Del had continued. ''When I first met him that boy was one of the angriest street fighters that ever got sent to the Double B.''

The pain had been acute, and she'd sunk her teeth into her bottom lip before she could help herself. When she opened her eyes again she saw Del's steady gaze still on her.

It had been on her throughout the whole procedure, Tess recalled, taking a final sip of her tea. It had been on her when she'd allowed him and Van Zane to help her to the couch, and it had darkened with concern when the surgeon had frowningly noted her limp.

She preferred not to remember what had come next, she thought with chagrin. While Daniel had kept watch over Connor in the spare room, Van Zane had whisked her back onto the pine table and had tended to her ignominious wound.

You were right, Connor, she thought, letting both her weariness and the low voices of the three friends at the table wash over her. *You said the Double B was where a person went when they came to the end of the line, and you were right. I don't know who these men are or what Del meant when he said you'd been one of the ranch's bad boys a long time ago...but I know we've reached sanctuary here.*

Sleep claimed her within minutes. And if at some point in her dreams that night a massive gray shape that could have been a man or could have been a wolf loomed up in front of her out of a dark roadway, she was too exhausted to care.

"WHAT IN THE *HELL* do you think you're doing?"

Hawkins still could peel paint off a wall with that parade-ground voice when he wanted, Connor thought, wincing as a brand-new headache overlaid the seemingly permanent one he'd woken up to this morning. He finished zipping the fly of his pants, and turned to the older man standing in the doorway of the bedroom.

"Getting up," he said curtly. "I've spent the past thirty-six hours lying flat on my back, and I've had enough, Del. What news do you have about the hunt for me and the woman and the kid? And where are they, anyway?"

"No news yet, and the woman and the kid are down at the corral with Daniel," his former mentor replied evenly. "If you're talking about the woman who saved your life and the kid who thinks you walk on water, that is."

Del's gaze lasered his. Connor looked away.

"I need a shave and a shirt to wear," he said. "Is there a razor I can use?"

"Razor's in the cabinet and I should be able to find some sweatshirts that might fit you." Del's tone was still crisp, but his gaze softened somewhat. "You think you screwed up, don't you? You think there should have been something more you could have done to keep them from this."

"To keep them from having to hide out while my area director, a fellow agent and a homeless wacko who's already killed two people hunt them down? You bet I should have done more," Connor agreed. "I should have reacted more quickly to those two phony agents. I should have picked up on something that might have given me a clue Jansen was dirty. I should—"

He stopped. Turning to the night table beside the

bed and trying not to lose his balance as he did, he grabbed his watch and began strapping it around his wrist.

"She was in to see me this morning," he muttered. "She looked pale. How is she?"

"Before Van left to catch his flight back to Philadelphia a few hours ago, he checked her over," Del replied. "He said she still should take it easy, but otherwise she's fine. Which you would have known if you hadn't pretended to be asleep when she looked in on you," he added.

When Connor remained silent, the older man pushed himself away from the doorway. "I'll rustle up those sweatshirts. And one last thing." He nailed Connor with a glance. "When Daniel and I knew John MacLeish, he wasn't a wacko, he was a damned hero. I'd appreciate it if you remembered that."

The frostiness had been back in Hawkins's tone, Connor thought as he made his way into the bathroom with just enough energy left to brace his hands on the rim of the sink and stand there. Frustration swept through him. At thirty-one a man's body wasn't supposed to slow him down, he told himself angrily. It was all very well for Van Zane to tell him he was coming along faster than he had any right to expect after what he'd been through, but he'd already lost a day and a half, dammit. He needed to be back to normal *now*.

You think you've got it tough? a voice in his head asked. *The ex-Marine who just left this room was in his twenties when he stepped on that booby trap and lost his legs. Until a few years ago he was confined to a wheelchair, and never once have you ever heard him complain that life dealt him a bum hand.*

Connor raised his head. In the mirror in front of him was a stubble-jawed man who looked as if he'd just come off a three-day bender. In the mirror was a man who was damned lucky to be alive and in one piece.

He knew that, just as he knew that Tess Smith was the only reason he was standing here at all. Why hadn't he wanted to talk to her when she'd come to see him earlier?

It was partly what Del had guessed, he thought, finding the razor and a can of shave cream in the medicine cabinet. He lathered his face and began shaving. She and Joey were in danger, and he couldn't help thinking he'd failed them in some way. But that wasn't all there was to it.

Even before Van Zane had told him, he'd known that it had been Tess's blood that had flowed into him, bringing him back from the brink of death. The surgeon hadn't minced words when describing his condition.

"Nearest thing to a corpse I've ever seen," he'd said when he'd come to say goodbye this afternoon. "For a few seconds I wasn't sure if I should continue prepping you or just stick a lily in your hands and be done with it. You were real, real gone, boy. More than halfway across the River Styx and getting ready to step onto the far shore."

So there was no way he could have been aware of anything that was going on around him, Connor thought, tapping the razor on the edge of the sink. There was no way, but still he'd known.

The images had already begun to fade when he'd briefly regained consciousness the first time. Now he could only remember the vaguest scraps of the hallucination or dream or whatever you wanted to call it that he'd had during those long, silent seconds when his life had hung in the balance and the scales that had been rushing down toward the side of oblivion slowly began to tilt back the other way....

He'd seen a woman with dark braids. Her eyes had been shadowed with sadness, and her lips had moved constantly, although he hadn't been able to hear what she was saying. Her hands had sketched pictures in the air in front of her, and from her fingertips had flown strands of fine thread.

He'd seen a young girl lying stiffly on a bed, her eyes squeezed shut. He'd seen the same young girl floating above the bed, her mouth wide open in a soundless scream.

He'd seen a ragged and endless trail of people walking, a woman looking up as someone appeared by the window of the car she was sitting in, lightning flashing from a black sky into the ground all around him.

There'd been more, but those images were the only ones that had stayed with him after he'd awoken to find himself in the Double B's downstairs bedroom, his shoulder bandaged and the mother of all headaches pounding through his head. Even the headache hadn't dulled his reaction to the dreams he'd had.

He'd known instinctively that they hadn't come

from his subconscious. He'd known with equal certainty that they'd come from hers.

And that was insane, of course, Connor told himself tightly. A bead of scarlet appeared suddenly on the cheek he was shaving, and he swore under his breath. It was insane and illogical and he didn't accept it. He owed Tess Smith his life, but that didn't mean he'd somehow caught a glimpse into her soul, because if he had, then it was equally possible that she'd caught a glimpse of—

"Del asked me to bring these in for—oh, sorry." She was standing by the bed, a pile of sweatshirts and jeans in her arms. "The door was open. I thought I'd leave them for you."

"Thanks." Connor felt immediately guilty for his inadequate response. *Thanks,* he thought in disgust. *Oh, hey, thanks for driving through the night and nearly being killed in a accident for me. Thanks for getting me to the one place I knew would be safe. And, yeah, thanks for the blood, too.*

No wonder Del had walked out on him. Had he really been stupid enough to ask why Tess had looked a little pale?

She'd deposited the clothes onto the bed. He stepped out of the bathroom, the razor in his hand dripping shave cream onto the pine plank floor.

"You saved my life," he said baldly. "I haven't had the chance to thank you properly for that, but..."

At his words she turned back, her hand on the door frame. The trite sentiment died in his throat as those amber-brown eyes waited for him to finish what he'd been saying.

Straight brows, straight nose. Unsmiling and, for the moment, straight mouth. Despite the tall tales she spun in her job, in her private life she wasn't a woman who played fast and loose with her convictions, Connor thought slowly. He hadn't realized that when he'd first met her. Now that he did, it explained why she'd taken such an insane chance as to go on the run with a child whom she felt was in danger.

She's the one. The thought came to him so clearly that for a moment he wondered if he'd spoken it. *You're going to let her get away, but she's the one, and you're always going to regret it. Right down to the last minute of the last hour of the last day of your life. She's the one.*

He blinked. She was still watching him. He lifted his uninjured shoulder in a faint shrug.

"…but thank you." It was still inadequate, but anything would be. Her straight mouth curved fractionally.

"That's good Dineh blood you've got in you now—almost enough to make you an honorary member of the People." She shook her head. "But not enough so that you can bleed it all out again. You've nicked yourself."

Belatedly Connor looked down at the razor in his hand, and it suddenly struck him what he must look like. "My mind wasn't on the job at hand," he said with an attempt at casualness. "I'll finish up more carefully."

"I'd better go."

Her reply was swift, and he realized that she'd taken his statement as a hint that he wanted to be alone. A few minutes ago he had, Connor admitted. But, hell, now that she was here it was probably a good idea to tell her what he'd decided to do about the Jansen situation.

"No, stay." He stepped back in front of the mirror and rinsed the razor. "That is, if you're okay talking to a man with half his face lathered and the other half bleeding."

"I'm okay with that, and I've got a few minutes. Daniel and Del are teaching Joey how to throw a lasso." Tess sat on the edge of the bed and looked with interest around the room. "This is nice. I guess the bunkhouse for the bad boys doesn't have as many comfortable touches as the main house, though."

Connor came close to nicking himself again. "Del's been blabbing, I see," he said. "What exactly did he tell you?"

"Everything," Tess said promptly. "About the Double B taking in a crop of teenage tearaways every year and giving them a chance to turn their lives around, about the fact that for most of them it's this or juvenile detention, about you and Tyler Adams and Jess somebody-or-other and Gabe Riggs being best buddies here fifteen years ago."

"Jess Crawford." Connor pressed the ball of his thumb to his jugular and scraped cautiously around it. "Thank God Del takes a much-needed breather in the summer months, or there'd be a dozen or so teenage tough guys here right now. Did he tell you about Tye and Susannah, Daniel's daughter?"

"A little." She sounded uncertain. "Tye ran a security firm out in California and when some threatening incidents started happening at the ranch, Del asked him to look into things here. The incidents were tied up with a man Susannah Bird had been running from for over a year, and when it was all over Tye asked Susannah if she'd marry him and let him be a father to her baby boy, Danny.''

Her voice had a smile in it. ''Of course she said yes. When Tye finishes winding up his business in California, they're going to build a house on Double B land, and he's going to help Del run the ranch. Del told me he wants to start having more time for himself and his own new wife.'' She raised her eyebrows. ''Is she the Greta Hassell who used to be a top model and is now a world-famous artist, Connor? Her work's amazing.''

''It is, isn't it? I told Hawkins at his wedding a few weeks ago that he got way luckier than he deserved when Greta tied the knot with him. Too bad she had an obligation she couldn't get out of this week at a gallery in New York,'' Connor said. ''Sounds like Del filled you in on everything.''

Something in his tone must have given him away, because out of the corner of his eye he saw her raise her head at him. He turned and met her gaze.

''Including the fact that Daniel just got out of prison last month for killing the man who raped and killed his wife years ago,'' she said steadily. ''It doesn't change my opinion of Daniel, Connor.''

''Which is?'' This wasn't the conversation he'd intended to have with her, Connor thought, but he was interested in hearing her opinion, not only on Daniel Bird but on Del Hawkins.

*And also you just like to hear her talk, right? That
husky voice of hers could be reciting the multiplica-
tion table and you'd be perfectly happy to stand here
and listen.*

With a flicker of irritation he dismissed the notion.
Turning on the taps with more force than was needed,
he rinsed the razor and replaced it in the medicine
cabinet.

"Why, I'd trust him with my life, of course." Her
tone was tinged with faint surprise. "Del, too. They
and Van Zane all served in Vietnam together, right?"

Seemingly Hawkins's confidences had stopped
short of revealing too many details of his own background, Connor thought cynically. He reached for the
towel behind him, and wiped a last fleck of shave
foam from his jawline.

"Del and Daniel were in the same outfit," he confirmed. "Van was the first medic to attend to Del after
the injury that cost him his legs, and Del's always
credited his medical skill with saving his life." He
slung the towel onto the rack and stepped out of the
bathroom. "I'd trust Del and Daniel, too. I'd never
met Van before yesterday but if Hawkins says he's
true blue, that's good enough for me."

"He won't report the gunshot wound, Connor,"
Tess said quietly. "He knows that could lead Jansen
right to us."

"Jansen, Leroy and MacLeish," Connor supple-
mented. He strode to the bed and picked up a sweatshirt. "The three of them have to be allied. It doesn't
make sense otherwise."

"No, it doesn't."

Now it was her tone that alerted him. Her amber-brown eyes met his reluctantly as he shoved the sweatshirt's wrists halfway up his forearms, realizing as he did so that the gesture stemmed from a need to ready himself for action.

"Hit me with it," he said flatly. "You've learned something that's changed the equation, haven't you?"

"I've learned something that's changed everything." Her voice took on an extra edge of huskiness. "I haven't told Del or Daniel yet. I thought you should hear it first."

It could only be one thing. Connor narrowed his gaze. "He's got his memory back," he guessed. "Joey's got his memory back, and he remembers how the hit in the alleyway went down, am I right?"

"Right about that," Tess said somberly. "But wrong about the way you and everyone else read the physical evidence at the murder scene." She shook her head. "Quayle showed up at that alleyway with the intention of killing MacLeish, Connor. And Mac only attacked Quayle when the retired agent realized there'd been a witness to the whole thing and tried to kill Joey."

Chapter Eight

"Maybe the John MacLeish you knew was a hero, Del," Connor said, pushing himself away from the verandah railing as if he needed a physical outlet for the frustration simmering just below the surface of his words. "But that was a long time ago. Something obviously snapped in the man during those five years he spent as a prisoner of war."

He shook his head. "Joey's story doesn't tally with the evidence. I don't think he's consciously lying, just that his imagination's gone into overtime."

She'd predicted this, Tess told herself tightly. Even during those few terrible minutes after the accident when she'd thought Connor was dead, she'd known with agonized honesty that he and she could never have been on the same side of any issue for long. This afternoon, after she'd told him what Joey had remembered, it had taken him all of two seconds to come up with an explanation that fit his rigid facts. And in the hours since, he'd stuck to it like glue.

He'd hidden his rampant disbelief from Joey while he was questioning him, though, and she was grateful for that. Not until the nine-year-old was in bed and the adults had taken their after-dinner coffee to the wraparound verandah had he resumed his objections, his attitude so antagonistic that it seemed almost as if—

"Sounds like you've got an agenda of your own here, Connor. A reason why you need to keep believing Mac's guilty."

Del had put her tenuous suspicion into words, she thought. His carved features made even stronger by the flicker of the citronella candle on the table beside him, he went on with a frown.

"Last time I looked we were still in the good old U.S. of A., and I always thought the rule was a man was innocent until a judge and jury said different."

"I don't have an agenda or a motive." Connor sounded impatient. "I leave that for you and Daniel. I just want to—"

"Back up there, Virge." Del's voice made it an order. "What the hell do you mean by that crack? What motive do you see us as having?"

"For God's sake, Del." The tension suddenly seeping from his posture, Connor slumped back against the railing, raking a hand through his hair. "Roll up your sleeve and take a look at those two bees fighting to the death you've got tattooed on your biceps. Mac-Leish was a comrade in arms, one of the original Double B's. You've never wanted to believe he could turn cold-blooded killer."

"I'm just a West Virginia mountain boy who spent the past fifteen years in prison, so maybe I got about as much right to give an opinion as Daisy here."

Soft as it was, Daniel Bird's drawl commanded attention. Tess glanced at him, seated a few feet away near the heeler hound bitch with her sleeping pups, but his head was bent. A small silvery blade glinted against the ball of his thumb as he continued whittling the chunk of pine he'd been working on since the conversation had started.

"But the way I see it, if the lieutenant here held with shielding a man just because he'd been a Double B, why would he have gone into the jungle after the fourth member of Beta Beta Force all those years ago? Why did he nearly give his own life to make sure Zeke Harmon never got the chance to kill again?"

Tess's patience came to an end.

"Fighting bees, someone named Harmon, tattoos— can anybody tell me what we're talking about?" She set down her mug of coffee. "I'd already guessed from the way Del was talking that he knew something of MacLeish's war record. Now it sounds to me like the connection was a whole lot stronger."

"As strong as it gets," Daniel said, glancing sideways at a silent Hawkins. "As strong as brothers. All four of us were, at the beginning."

"Until Harmon broke the bond, and destroyed Beta Beta Force," Connor said. "If it happened once it could happen again, Del, and you know it."

"Harmon didn't break the bond," Del said. "There never was one, as far as he was concerned." He looked away from Connor and toward Tess, his expression softening. "It's an old story, sweetheart. You sure you want to hear it?"

"I'm Dineh," she said evenly. "We like our stories. What was Beta Beta Force?"

"A four-man covert operations group." Del leaned forward in his chair and laced his fingers together loosely. "We took on the jobs that no one else wanted, went deeper in-country than the regular forces could. It seems a lifetime ago now."

"It seems like yesterday."

Daniel's tone was low. Glancing at him, she saw the darkly gleaming line on the ball of his thumb before he quickly wiped it on his jeans and resumed his whittling. Del's gaze sharpened in concern for his old friend before he went on.

"The four members were me, Daniel, Mac and Harmon. And Daniel's right—at first we were as close as brothers. Any one of us knew that the man beside him would fight to the death for him, which was what the tattoos were supposed to symbolize."

Against the railing Connor shifted. Tess caught the compassion that crossed his features before they became remote again.

"At some point rumors began to circulate about a rogue killer who was murdering for his own pleasure, right?" he said. "Civilians, the enemy, your own soldiers—it didn't matter who, and the murders were performed as sadistically as possible. The Double B's were assigned to track down the killer."

"We were assigned to track down the killer," Del agreed. His laced fingers tightened. "And we found he was one of us."

Del had said it seemed a lifetime ago, but it was obvious from the raw betrayal in his voice that the events he was recounting were still fresh in his mind. A man he'd trusted had proven to be a monster. It was hard to imagine the pain that revelation had caused him.

But she didn't have to imagine it. She knew exactly how that kind of pain felt, she thought numbly.

"We turned Zeke in to the authorities." Daniel closed the blade of the jackknife and slipped it into his pocket. "Day after, they up and shipped me home. Said they were disbanding us on account of the war coming to an end, but I knew that weren't why. They wanted to pretend we never existed."

He lifted his shoulders. "When they found they needed Beta Beta Force one last time, it was just Del and Mac."

"Harmon had escaped custody." Del's grin was mirthless. "Since he could melt into the jungle like a ghost, the brass knew only a Double B stood a chance of finding him, so they sent Mac and me after him. We split up, I found Harmon first, and I shot him. A second later the world blew up around me."

He shrugged. "He'd rigged a booby trap. When his body was recovered the official report was that my bullet had taken him in the heart, so I guess he was dead before my foot sprung the bomb. That's not important. What is important is that John found me and carried me back to base camp and that crazy miracle worker Van Zane, twenty-five miles on his back."

The gaze he directed at Connor was hard. "So tell me again why I should believe the man who saved my life is a stone killer? I'm still having trouble wrapping my mind around that one."

"Because two days after that trek through the jungle, John MacLeish got captured by the enemy. Because he spent five years in what they called a tiger cage—a bamboo cage not big enough for a man to stand up or lie down in—while the outside world didn't know if he was dead or alive." Connor took a breath. "Yeah, he was finally released and came back a hero, Del, and yeah, for a while it seemed as if he'd put what had happened behind him. He married a Vietnamese woman. From all accounts they were very much in love. About ten years ago he decided to enter politics, and with his war record he probably would have been a shoo-in as his party's candidate in the next senatorial race. But then he snapped."

"I thought the name sounded familiar, but I didn't make the connection," Tess said slowly. "It was a big news story, wasn't it? He killed his wife, and then supposedly committed suicide by throwing himself into the Rio Grande."

"But his body was never recovered, and now we know why." Connor rubbed his jaw wearily. "Dammit, Del, they dumped this case in my lap because I'd been looking into that ten-year-old case *before* Quayle was killed and the murderer's prints came back as MacLeish's—a man who had been presumed to be dead. And I'd been looking into it at your request, remember?"

"Because of that Scudder business and Daniel turning up again after all these years." Del nodded grudgingly. "I figured if one old friend I'd always been told had died was really alive, Mac might be, too. But even then I made no secret of the fact that I didn't believe he'd killed Huong, his wife. You weren't completely convinced he had, either.''

"My initial look at the police file raised some doubts," Connor agreed. "But there's no doubt now that MacLeish killed both Huong and Quayle—and despite what Joey says about his pal, that second murder couldn't have been self-defense. I still don't know what Quayle was doing in that alleyway, but I do know that he showed up unarmed, Del.''

"Quayle was shot," Tess interjected. "You told me that yourself. It's more likely that an ex-FBI agent would be equipped with a gun than to assume the weapon belonged to a man who took his meals at soup kitchens. Mac might have had a knife with him, but not something he could sell for a decent street price, like a gun. It had to be Quayle's. It couldn't have been—''

"You told me I let myself be boxed in by facts and logic," Connor said. "I guess I do, at that. One of the facts that makes up this particular box is a ballistics test, dammit. Quayle was shot with the same gun that killed Huong MacLeish ten years ago—a gun that was registered as belonging to Mac.''

"Why didn't you tell us this at the start?" Del's posture was rigid as he spoke, and Tess saw the sinews in his neck standing out like cords. Beside her she was aware of Daniel getting to his feet. A tremor ran through the big West Virginian's body before he turned on his heel and walked into the house, the screen door slamming shut behind him.

"Because I didn't want to be the son of a bitch who totally destroyed your faith in a man who used to be a hero,'' Connor said hoarsely. ''I know how much the Double B bond means to you and Daniel. I'd hoped the two of you would come to see there was a possibility MacLeish wasn't the person you remembered, but this evening I realized that wasn't going to happen—not after Joey's version of events bolstered your hopes that your old buddy had no choice but to kill Quayle in order to save a child's life.''

He exhaled. Watching him, Tess knew with sudden certainty that there was something more he'd been keeping from them, and cold anger flashed through her.

Connor might have meant well, but he'd handled this all wrong. How could he not have mishandled it? she thought. The wall he kept around himself not only ensured that others couldn't get close to him, it made it impossible for Virgil Connor to reach out successfully to anyone else—even the man who had given him back his life not once, but twice now.

And if he can't let Del in, it's no use hoping he could ever open himself to you. Yes, he kissed you, and yes, you've caught him looking at you once or twice. You were looking, too, this afternoon when he was standing there in a pair of pants and not much else. But that's just physical, and as good as physical might be between the two of you, don't let yourself believe there could be anything more. Not with Connor.

Very carefully she grasped her mug of coffee. It was cold. She raised it to her lips, anyway.

What dark tunnel had that train of thought emerged from? she wondered shakily. She barely knew the man. She could admire his dedication to his job, and his courage had undoubtedly saved both her life and Joey's, but there was no real common ground between the two of them.

Besides, he was hiding something from her. Whatever it was, it was obvious he saw this situation as a one-man operation, with him making all the decisions and taking all responsibility for Joey's safety. How Connor managed to work with a partner was a mystery to her, Tess thought in frustration. Paula Geddes had to be an exceptional woman to put up with—

The sip of cold coffee she'd swallowed stuck in her throat. She set the mug back on the table, slopping some of the liquid on her hand in the process.

"You've contacted her." She could hear the barely suppressed fury in her voice, but she didn't care. "After I told you what Joey had remembered you contacted Geddes and told her where we were, didn't you? You knew Del and Daniel and I would find it harder than ever to believe in MacLeish's guilt, and you needed someone else with the same just-the-facts-ma'am methods to help—"

"Just the facts, ma'am? Most of the time our Virgil accuses me of being too imaginative, but coming from him, I take it as a compliment."

The wry admission came from the woman who'd just rounded the corner of the verandah. Her slim figure was garbed in a navy-blue pantsuit, a braided gold bangle on one wrist providing the only note of ornamentation to her outfit, and her hair was cropped close to her head in tight spirals. The light from the citronella candle couldn't completely erase the weary shadows purpling the coffee-colored skin under her eyes.

"I told you not to spring me on them as a surprise, Connor."

Under the navy jacket the woman's shoulders lifted in a frustrated shrug. She extended her hand to Tess.

"I hear you once battled Bigfoot and won. More to the point, I hear you did a better job of protecting Joey than I did when he came to you the night the safe house was blown. It's an honor to meet you, Tess."

Her handclasp was warm and firm. Tess knew her own was little more than a light grasp, although that wasn't due to antagonism but to her heritage, she acknowledged. The People had never really taken to the habit of touching the hands of strangers upon first meeting them. But then again, this woman wasn't a complete stranger.

"My apologies, Tess." As if she'd read her mind, the woman released her hand. "You're Dineh, and I should have known better. By the way, I'm Paula Geddes, Connor's partner."

"BREACH OF SECURITY?" As Paula spoke, Tess saw her shake her head before the female agent tore off another chunk of the bread at the side of her bowl and sopped up the last morsel of chili in the bowl in front of her. "Don't worry, Del, the Double B's harder to get into than Fort Knox. When Daniel stopped at the gate on his way out I was being grilled by a very suspicious young man who was holding a rifle on me."

"Joseph Tahe." Del grinned. "He's one of Joanna and Matt Tahe's cousins. Joanna's a nurse who runs a new-mother's clinic on the Dinetah, and her brother, Matt, is Tribal Police. When we had some problems here last month I asked him to suggest a couple of men I could hire as security."

The ex-Marine had taken to Paula Geddes almost immediately, Tess noted, but that wasn't so surprising. What was surprising was that she herself felt no reticence with Paula. The woman was obviously in her late forties—in the well-lit kitchen the lines of experience bracketing her mouth and accentuating those dark eyes were plainly visible—but her attitude was less stiff than her younger partner's.

As if in illustration of exactly that, Connor scowled. "Daniel gave Joseph the okay to let you through? Come to that, just where the hell was he heading at this time of night, anyway?"

"Cool it, Virge," Paula sighed. Tess hid a smile. It was apparent that behind that sigh lay more than a few previous head buttings with her by-the-book partner. "After I showed Daniel my ID he asked me questions about the phone call I made to you just after Jansen's goons tried to kill you at the motel two nights ago—questions pointed enough that I knew you'd given him some details about our conversation. My answers satisfied him that I really was who I said I was. As to where he was going, how should I know?"

"Last Chance." From Del's curt tone it was clear Connor was still in Dutch with him. "Earlier today Daniel said he might drop round to the café in town to see if anyone was talking about mysterious visitors to the Double B." He rubbed his jaw. "As far as I know, no one saw us hauling you into the pickup the night of the accident, but he thought it wouldn't hurt to get up to speed on the local gossip, if there is any."

Paula threw Connor a glance and then turned to Tess. "The way I heard it from my less-than-forthcoming partner, you had a little tire trouble on the way here. It sounds like it might have been a tad more than that, if he had to be pulled from the wreckage. What happened?" Her manner was suddenly serious. "Dear God, had the car been tampered with?"

Tess shook her head. "It had nothing to do with Petrie and Malden. A tire blew, but the accident was mainly my fault. I swerved to avoid a—"

The scene—and why hadn't she remembered it before now? she wondered in confusion—dropped joltingly into place in her memory, like a photographic slide that had been stuck and had suddenly been released in front of the beam of a projector. It filled the screen of her mind—the dark road, the headlights, the sudden shape looming up directly in the path of the sedan.

Except there was something wrong with the memory, Tess thought worriedly. Everything had happened so fast, but a handful of details had seared themselves into her brain. She'd seen a flash of white teeth. She'd seen a yellow eye. She'd seen bristling gray hair.

It had been too big. And it had walked upright.

"I...I swerved to avoid hitting an animal," she

said faintly. "It looked like a wolf. Or maybe some kind of dog."

A wolf or a dog leaping desperately to get out of the way of the rushing death bearing down on it. That sounded right. That might have been what had given her the impression that the creature she'd seen in the instant before she'd jerked the sedan's steering hard over had walked like a man.

It had been an animal. It *hadn't* been—

"You were going in to a meeting with Jansen when I called you on your cell this afternoon, Paula."

Beside Tess, Connor tipped his chair back and drummed impatient fingers on the scarred pine of the table. His hand brushed against hers and for a moment his fingers stilled, his touch warm against the coldness that had spread through her. He moved his hand away, his attention directed at his partner.

"How did it go? Did you get the impression he suspected you'd been in contact with me?"

"That was what the meeting was about—he called in every agent who had more than just a nodding acquaintance with you, me included—and warned us there was a possibility you might try to sell them the story you'd been set up. He took me aside afterward to remind me that I was still on medical leave, and that he didn't like me getting involved in the investigation."

Geddes frowned. "He's good, Connor. Really good. If he hadn't made that one tiny slip when he came to see me at the hospital and if I hadn't remembered it when I overheard those agents talking about

the armed-and-dangerous alert on you, even I might
have fallen for his act today.''

''What slip?''

She needed to ground herself in the normalcy of
this discussion, Tess thought as she ventured the
question. Not that an FBI agent getting framed by a
dirty area director was normal, exactly, but there had
to be some logic behind Jansen's actions, if only they
could figure it out. And logic was comforting. Logic
was dependable. Knowing there were immutable rules
that kept the universe from spinning nightmarishly
out of control meant that she hadn't—*couldn't* have—
seen what she'd imagined she'd seen two nights ago.

It wasn't logical that Connor's touch a moment ago
had taken away some of the iciness that had gripped
her. She didn't for a moment believe he'd sensed her
state of mind and had instantly acted to reassure her,
but logical or not, he'd taken the edge off her panic
enough so that her question hadn't sounded out of
place.

Del raised inquiring eyebrows at Paula as he lifted
a tin coffeepot from the cookstove. She held out her
mug before replying to Tess.

''I wasn't even supposed to be on duty the night
the safe house was blown. Terry Frakes was Bill Danzig's partner, but it was Terry and his wife's first wedding anniversary. Weeks before we'd pulled this assignment he'd booked reservations at an expensive
restaurant.''

Her grin was rueful. ''My husband spent our an-
niversaries at racetracks or in poker games, which is
why I divorced him, but Terry's a sweetheart. I told

him I'd cover for him, even though it meant spending twelve hours with Rick Leroy.''

She pursed her lips dismissively. ''Rick has a problem with women. He has a bigger problem with African-Americans. So while I was playing cards with Bill at a penny a point and beating the pants off him, he was on the other side of the room dividing his time between ogling *News at Eleven*'s blond anchor babe and glowering at the woman of color he'd been forced to work with. Joey had been in bed for about two hours by then, and I'd looked in on him once or twice. Everything seemed normal enough until Rick went into the kitchen, saying he was going to make himself a sandwich. That's when the lights went out in the apartment.''

Slim brown fingers wrapped around the coffee mug in front of her. A faint tremor ran through them.

''It gets hazy after that. I know I grabbed my gun from the table beside me. Bill seemed under the impression that something Rick had done in the kitchen had blown an electrical circuit, because he yelled out words to that effect. That's when I got shot.''

Some of the tension left her. ''My ex always said I was one pigheaded, thick-skulled woman. I guess he was right. The doctors told me the bullet grazed my skull instead of penetrating it and killing me instantly.''

Carelessly she reached up and tugged at the tight curls on her head. The curls lifted off, revealing her lopsidedly shaven head and the white band of surgical gauze.

''No way was I going out looking like this,'' Paula

drawled. "A girl's got some pride. The wig's not bad, is it?"

Any last reserve that Tess had felt dissipated. Now that she'd met the woman, she was glad Geddes was involved. Tough, good-humored, and courageous, not only would she be able to report back on Jansen's movements, but she also might be more open-minded than Connor had been about Mac's possible innocence.

"You said Jansen slipped up," Del prompted, his smile still lingering as Paula tossed the wig into her open purse on the floor beside her. She nodded at the purse.

"He played Mr. Nice Guy, retrieving my shoulder bag from the safe house to give it to me when he came to the hospital. Frankly, the only possession I'd been worried about was this—" she touched the gold bangle on her wrist "—since it was a family heirloom. The nursing staff had removed it for safekeeping, thank God," she added. "But getting back to Jansen. When he gave me my purse he made a little joke about my fifty-seven cents worth of winnings that he'd found at the scene being all there in my change purse if I wanted to check."

"Winnings?" Tess's brow cleared. "Oh. From the penny-a-point game with Danzig."

"Yeah." Paula's gaze darkened. "The thing is, I didn't tell Jansen I'd been beating Bill in that game. So the only way he could have known it was if he'd learned it from—"

"If he'd learned it from Leroy," Connor said harshly. "Dammit, what's their angle? What's their connection to Quayle and MacLeish, and why is it so important for them to make sure Joey never remembers what he saw in that alleyway?''

''Joey *has* remembered,'' Del said sharply, shoving back his chair and getting to his feet with an effort. ''It's time for me to take one last turn around the barns,'' he muttered, opening the cupboard over the kitchen counter where he'd earlier informed Tess he kept a couple of flashlights for just this nightly chore. ''I need some fresh air any—aw, *hell.*''

The curse came from him in an undertone. Glancing quickly at him, Tess saw him thrust a scrap of paper at Connor.

''Daniel left a note in the cupboard for me to find,'' he said shortly. ''The damn fool's taken it upon himself to go to Albuquerque and find MacLeish.''

Chapter Nine

It was no use, Tess thought. She couldn't sleep, and it wasn't the coffee she'd had after supper that was keeping her awake, or the arrival of Paula Geddes, who'd accepted Del's offer to stay the night and was presumably having no trouble sleeping in the bedroom Tess had shown her to three hours ago when the household had retired for the night.

It wasn't even her worry over Daniel. She swung her bare feet to the floor.

Connor's refusal to entertain the possibility that MacLeish might have acted in self-defense had nothing to do with the ballistics report he'd cited as his clinching proof—it couldn't have, she thought in exasperation, since he himself was now a victim of Jansen's trumped-up evidence—and everything to do with his personal attitude toward Joey's story.

His attitude toward Joey, and his attitude toward her, she reflected, feeling her way down the shadowed stairs to the main floor of the house. She held her breath as she passed the closed door of the spare bedroom that had been allocated to Connor, letting it out only when she reached the kitchen.

Joey had transferred some of his hero-worship of her to the man he'd initially been so hostile toward. The fact that Connor had been shot had seemingly brought home to the boy that the agent was ready to put his life on the line for him.

And the fact that the great Tess Smith had turned out to be his aunt and someone who made sure he washed behind his ears in the mornings had definitely changed her status, she told herself dryly, although he'd taken the news of their relationship with an equanimity that had surprised her.

"You're mom's sister?"

He'd been sitting on the porch at the time, and he'd bent his face to the squirming puppy in his lap. For a moment she'd wondered whether she might not have been wiser to withhold the information until her nephew's life was in less turmoil. Then he'd looked up at her.

"Does that mean I don't have to get fostered out anymore?" His manner had been studiedly casual. "'Cause I'm tired of that, Tess. I want to stay in one place with one family."

With equal casualness she'd nodded, knowing a demonstrative reaction from her would be too much for him at that point. "That's what it means. You okay with that?"

"I guess." His tough-guy reply had been spoiled by the exuberant whoop he'd given a moment later as he'd raced off the porch, the puppy still cradled in his arms.

She hadn't had to tell the Hangar 61 story for at least twenty-four hours now, Tess realized with a mixture of relief and faint regret. But several times today she'd seen Joey shadowing Connor and had heard him asking the agent innumerable questions about cases he'd been on, how many times he'd had to fire a gun, how old someone had to be to join the Bureau…

Opening the refrigerator door and pulling out the milk, she repressed a grin. Connor had worn the same harassed expression she'd seen on Daisy when the heeler hound mama had been trying to escape her scampering pups and have a few moments of peace and quiet to herself. But when Tess had taken pity on him, he'd shrugged aside her offer to keep Joey out of his way.

"He's not bothering me." A rare smile had briefly creased one tanned cheek. "Well, not much, anyway. And Del and Daniel said when they'd rested up from the lasso lesson they gave him earlier, they would show him how to saddle a horse. Between the three of us we should be able to wear him out before bedtime."

There'd been rough affection in his tone. Virgil Connor might try to hide it, but it was obvious he cared for the child he'd sworn to protect, Tess thought, pouring herself a glass of milk. She pulled out one of the hoopbacked chairs that ringed the pine table, and paused indecisively. He cared for Joey. And he felt something toward her. What that something was she wasn't exactly sure, just as she wasn't sure what it was she felt about him.

"A little plain, old-fashioned lust and a whole lot of irritation, most of the time," she said out loud as she unlatched the kitchen door and stepped out onto the porch. "Which makes Agent Connor the equivalent of eating cheese just before bedtime. It keeps you awake, makes you cranky and gives you *very* disturbing dreams. Face it—he's the reason why you're wandering around in the middle of the night instead of—"

"Good, you're here." The glass of milk nearly slipped through her fingers as the voice came out of the darkness. "Because if you hadn't shown up in the next five minutes I'd about decided to go wake you up. Since I'm not sure which room's yours, Del could have been in for a shock."

"Either that or you would have found the right room," Tess said, hoping her tone was sharp enough to mask her still-twanging nerves. "Then you would have been the one to get a shock, Connor. Del gave me a key to the nightstand drawer, and I keep my little derringer in there. What's so urgent you couldn't wait to talk to me tomorrow?"

"Nothing, I suppose." His voice was edged. "Everything. Hell, I don't know."

By now her eyes had adjusted to the starlight that was the only illumination on the verandah. Connor was sitting in a chair, his legs thrust out in front of him and a tumbler of some gold-colored liquid on the chair's wide arm by his elbow. He was wearing one of the pairs of jeans he'd borrowed earlier—Del had told her they were Tye's—but what he was wearing up top could only have belonged to Virgil Connor.

Who owned undershirts anymore? Tess thought incredulously, stepping over his outstretched legs and taking the chair beside him. And who wore them under white polyester shirts, for God's sake? Because that must have been the case—he certainly hadn't shown up here with a change of clothes, so the undershirt would have been what he'd been wearing when he'd been shot.

Ridiculously, it was the last straw.

"Everything," she repeated flatly. "Nothing. What's with you? You know, if I did believe in aliens I'd find it entirely possible that one of these days you'd be returning to your mothership. You screwed up tonight with Del and Daniel. Your partner has to bite her tongue to keep from losing her patience with you. Every so often I find myself starting to like you, and then you do or say something so incredibly *wrong* that I wonder if you've got any inkling of how to deal with people."

She took a breath. "And that undershirt's insane, especially with the damn shoulder holster."

Not her most coherent few moments, she thought as she sputtered into silence. But he'd gotten the point.

"I know I screw up." His bandaged shoulder lifted and fell. "I know I don't interact well. When I was a kid I used to solve that problem with my fists, but my year at the Double B taught me fighting wasn't the answer."

He took a swallow of the liquid in his glass. "Van Zane told me no liquor," he said thoughtfully. "You think that includes a watered-down shot of rum?"

"Probably." She shook her head. "I was right that

night in the motel, wasn't I? About the kind of life
you lead, I mean.''

"No real friends, married to the job, empty apartment?" He glanced sideways at her. "I have friends.
I keep in touch with Tyler and Gabe. Jess Crawford
and I always rubbed each other the wrong way, but I
saw him just last month.''

"You saw him last month when that Scudder business was taking place here," Tess said. "And although you saw Tye then, too, before that you hadn't
seen or heard from him for years. As for Gabriel
Riggs, Del says that ever since last year when a kid-
nap recovery assignment he was handling went bad
and the hostage was killed, Gabe's dropped out of
sight.''

"And just how did this conversation with Del come
about?" Connor set his glass down. "Were you
pumping him for information about me?"

"No." She let her one-word answer lie there. After
a moment she heard him exhale.

"Sorry." He frowned. "I felt like a damned heel
tonight, Tess. I owe Del a lot. I wanted to tell him I
thought Mac was still the hero he used to be, but I
couldn't lie to him."

He tossed back the remainder of the rum and went
on, his voice roughened by the liquor. "I owe you,
too. Hell, I've got your blood in my veins, and if that
doesn't put me in your debt I don't know what does.
But I can't believe Joey's story.''

"Why not?" She saw him open his mouth to answer her, and she forestalled him with an impatient
movement of her hand. "Don't give me the ballistics

angle, Connor. Your area director is up to his neck in this—he was in touch with Leroy after the safe house hit, which means he wanted Joey silenced. But since he didn't silence him in time he's now going after you as well, just to make sure whatever it is he's afraid Joey saw in that alleyway never comes to light. I'm probably a secondary target, since with my dubious journalistic reputation Jansen doesn't have to worry much about me being believed.''

"Dubious rep—'' Connor stopped. "The *Eye-Opener* byline. Bigfoot. Hangar 61.''

"That'll do for starters.'' She bit her lip. "But I'm not the key player here, Joey is. Suspend your disbelief long enough to ask yourself what it would mean if Quayle really attacked MacLeish first, and Mac was forced to kill him to save a nine-year-old child. What if—again, let the ballistics report go for a minute—what if Quayle himself brought the gun that eventually killed him in the alleyway? If all that were true, how would you be approaching this case?''

"Dammit, the gun was registered to MacLeish. He shot his wife to death with it ten years ago. How do I disregard that?''

"The same way I disregard that undershirt you're wearing,'' Tess snapped. "With great difficulty, but I'm trying.''

"And I'm trying to overlook the fact that you're wearing a T-shirt that doesn't leave much to the imagination and a female version of boxer shorts,'' Connor ground out. He rubbed his jaw. "All right. If all that were true, I guess I'd be approaching this case as—''

He stopped. Tess crossed her arms over her chest,

annoyed with herself for letting his remarks about her attire throw her.

"As what?"

"As the attempted murder of John MacLeish," he said slowly. "And I'd be looking into the circumstances of his supposed suicide ten years ago, just in case this was the second time someone had tried to kill him."

He was silent for a second, and then he grunted dismissively. "You're hanging all this on Joey's story, and I won't buy Joey's story. I can't."

"You never say you *don't* buy his story," Tess retorted, stung to frustration. "You say you can't or you won't. That sounds like you're not allowing yourself to. That sounds like you're afraid to."

"Damn straight I'm not allowing myself to buy it." His voice was even sharper than hers had been. "Kids are unreliable witnesses. I know that from firsthand experience. I know that because twenty-one years ago *I—*"

Abruptly he got to his feet. Turning away from her, he stared out into the night, the set of his shoulders tense. Faint starlight picked out the gleam of oiled leather cutting the whiteness of the bandage on his upper arm and delineated the heavy swell of his biceps.

Tess stood. She took a step toward him. "You were in Joey's position once? You were a child witness to a crime?"

"Of the death of my father." His voice was a low rasp. "And I was convinced I'd seen something that never happened. It was years before the real memory came back.''

''How did he die?''

Somehow she'd guessed Virgil Connor didn't have parents still living, Tess thought. From the first he'd given the impression of being a man alone, a man who, if he'd ever known the reassurance of a core family unit, had had it taken from him long ago.

I don't interact well… How could he? she thought. He'd never learned how. The nearest thing Connor had to a family was the Double B, but even Del couldn't take the place of a father and a mother.

''He was a cop. He was shot while trying to prevent a bank robbery one day when he was off duty. I was with him at the time and I saw the whole thing.'' His back still to her, Connor took a deep breath. ''When I was questioned about what I'd witnessed, I insisted I'd seen my father put his own gun to his temple and pull the trigger. I said he'd committed suicide.''

''Why?'' The shocked question came from her in a gasp. She took a step closer, and he turned his head to look at her.

''Because that's how I remembered it,'' he said harshly. ''My memories of everything else that happened gibed with the other witnesses, but when it came to the part where my father pulled his gun to take down one of the robbers as they were racing out of the bank, my story suddenly became pure fantasy. Everyone else saw him take down one of the fleeing robbers and then get shot in his turn by the second robber. I saw him pull his gun and kill himself.''

He looked away again. ''My mother had died in a

car accident about a year before, and her death had torn him apart. I probably came up with that particular scenario because I'd become convinced in the months since she died that my father didn't want to live without her.''

''You'd been afraid he might kill himself. So when he was shot in front of your eyes, some part of you thought your worst fears had come true,'' Tess said softly. ''But eventually you remembered what had actually happened in the bank that day?''

''Oh, yeah, it came back eventually. Just like one of these days Joey'll probably remember what really happened in the alleyway.'' Connor shook his head. ''He'll remember that MacLeish shot Quayle in cold blood and forget his fantasies about Skinwalker. Looking back now, I recall every detail.''

''You don't have to talk about it.''

No matter that his father's death had occurred so long ago, she thought sadly, there were some things that never got easy. He'd convinced her. She had no choice but to accept that it was possible Joey's version of what had happened the day Quayle had been killed had sprung from his imagination.

''I haven't talked about it.'' Connor pushed himself away from the railing. ''Not since the real memory came back. I probably should have told someone, just to prove to myself I could. We were heading out to Fenway Park to catch a ball game, but first my father needed to stop at the bank to cash a check.''

''Fenway?'' Tess wrinkled her brow. ''Boston, right?''

''Boston's where I'm from, originally. After my

father's death I was sent to live with my aunt and uncle in New Mexico, but when my year at the Double B was up I didn't go back to them.'' Connor shrugged. ''Nice enough people, but I never fit in. I didn't return here until I was posted to the Albuquerque field office a year or so ago.''

Which explained why he hadn't known much about her culture, Tess thought. She listened as he went on.

''We'd barely walked into the bank when the holdup started. One of the robbers ordered everyone to hit the floor. My father shoved me down and then he got down, too. Like I say, I remember every detail. The floor was terrazzo, and I can still see the flecks of stone in the tiles. We were a few feet away from the loan manager's desk, and I recall seeing her staring at us from underneath it. She knew my father was a cop, and I saw him give her a reassuring nod of his head while we were lying there.''

He fell silent for a moment. From farther along the verandah Tess heard a faint snuffling noise as one of Daisy's pups moved closer to the comfort of his mama.

''There's not much else to tell.'' Connor sighed. ''The robbers released the teller and began backing toward the bank's doors. That's when my father got to his feet and went for his gun—I guess with everyone else still flat on the ground at that point, he realized there was no chance of an innocent bystander getting caught in the crossfire. He killed one of the robbers, and the one who killed him was taken down by the police as he burst out of the doors onto the street.''

"The police?" Tess blinked. "How did they know a robbery was in progress?"

"What?" Connor frowned, and then his brow cleared. "Oh. Because of the silent alarm." He saw her confusion and elaborated. "The one by the leg of the loan officer's desk. When my father gave her that nod, she pushed it."

He had no idea what he'd just said, Tess thought in shock. Virgil Connor *had* seen his father commit suicide—maybe not commit it consciously, maybe with no clear intent of doing so when he'd risen from the floor and pulled a gun on two desperate men— but whatever had been in the man's mind at the time, he'd taken the one course of action that had been almost certain to result in his own death.

His own unnecessary death, she thought. Connor's father had been well aware that the men racing out of the bank would run straight into the arms of the police.

The boy Connor had once been had known all that. That knowledge had made such a devastating impact on him at the time that he'd translated it into a vision of a man putting a gun to his own head, and when that vision had proven too much for him to endure he'd told himself it had been a complete lie.

Which was why he couldn't allow himself to buy Joey's story. Because if he bought Joey's, he would no longer be able to reject his own.

So what are you waiting for? It's only been possible for him to avoid the truth all these years because he hasn't spoken about it, but Connor's not blind. Ask him if he realizes that he's blanked out the detail about the alarm. Force him to face what it means, for heaven's sake.

The voice in her head was firm and decisive…but the voice in her head was wrong, Tess thought heavily. He needed to come to the truth by himself for it to release him.

"Paula's heading back to Albuquerque early tomorrow." His tone held enough briskness to indicate that the previous discussion had ended. "I think you and Del should sit in on the meeting I intend to have with her before she leaves. We need to clear the air over this MacLeish matter."

Maybe Paula could convince him to give Joey's story the benefit of the doubt. It was worth a shot.

"A meeting's probably a good idea." She forced a small smile. "I'd better get some sleep, I suppose."

"Yeah, I should be turning in soon, too." He gestured toward the holstered gun he was wearing. "Before I do I might take a run up to the gate, give Joseph Tahe a break for a while. 'Night, Tess."

"Good night, Connor."

She was halfway down the length of the verandah before he called out her name. She turned to see him still standing by the railing, a faint frown on his features.

"Why did you swerve the night of the accident, Tess? I could tell you didn't want to talk about it earlier, but now it's just you and me. What did you see?"

"I saw Skinwalker." She met his gaze without flinching. "I know you don't believe me, Connor. In spite of what I've said about keeping an open mind, when it came right down to it I didn't want to believe it, either. But I saw Skinwalker. I saw him as plain as I'm seeing you now.''

"Oh, for God's—'' He crossed the space between them, his brows drawing swiftly together. ''What do you mean, you didn't want to believe in Skinwalker? Of course you wanted to. Maybe you see that belief as a way of connecting to a heritage you never had the chance to know, maybe you think you'd be letting Joey down if you didn't accept his story about a monster. But you wanted to believe. And now you've convinced yourself, dammit.''

His gaze narrowed. ''Tell me, in those conversations you've had with Del the past couple of days, did he mention Alice Tahe? Is that part of all this— the fact that Matt and Joanna's great-grandmother warned Del something evil was threatening the ranch, an evil she says goes by the name of Skinwalker?''

"Del told me Matt and Joanna had a great-grandmother named Alice Tahe,'' Tess replied, her tone flat. ''He didn't tell me she'd warned him that Skinwalker's evil threatened the Double B. That's something else I wish I hadn't learned.''

Tipping her head to one side, she surveyed him with a quizzical look. ''You want to know why I work for the *Eye-Opener,* Connor? It's because I decided that if I wasn't going to be believed when I told the truth, I might as well make up the most outrageous lies I can think of and get paid for them. But I don't lie to myself. Whatever your logic and reason say, I didn't convince myself I saw something on that road two nights ago that wasn't really there.''

She stepped away from him. "I'm going to bed."

This time her hand was on the latch of the screen door when he spoke, his voice so low she had to strain to hear his words.

"I don't know how I kept missing it. He saw her push it, didn't he? Hell, he gave her the signal. He knew there wasn't any damn need for him to—"

Slowly Tess turned. Crystal-gray eyes met hers across a distance of a few yards, but even the distance and the darkness and the faint starlight weren't enough to obscure the glittering pain in Connor's shattered gaze.

"I did see him kill himself, didn't I?" he whispered hoarsely. "God help me, I saw exactly what I said I did, all those years ago."

Chapter Ten

"You realize this spins our investigation off into a whole different direction?" Paula asked. "I'm not saying that's a bad thing, Connor," she added. "Maybe looking at this from a new perspective will give us a handle on Jansen's motives."

Connor's partner was handling his surprising about-face from the evening before with aplomb, Tess thought. Del's eyebrows had risen in disbelief when the planned morning meeting between the four of them had started with Connor's announcement that he'd reconsidered Joey's story about Mac's actions in the alleyway.

She would have to come up with an explanation if Del asked her about Connor's change of heart, she told herself. She'd seen a man come to some hard truths last night—truths not only about himself, but about the man who had fathered him and loved him…and who had made a spur-of-the-moment decision that had left his young son alone and devastated.

"You'll never know everything that went through his mind when he stood up to take that shot, Connor," she'd said softly last night. "Maybe right at the last moment he thought he *could* take them both down. Maybe he thought a confrontation with the police outside posed more risk to civilians."

His expression had been bleak. "I do know my mother was the light of his life, and when he lost her all the lights went out for him. They went out for me, too, for a while."

He'd held the screen door open for her. "The ballistics report is hard evidence. But I'm willing to admit Joey's evidence could be just as valid. I'll ask Paula to check into Huong MacLeish's murder, see if she can spot any loose ends."

She'd nodded, not trusting herself to speak. Connor had brought his hand to her face, his palm to her cheek and his thumb brushing the corner of her mouth.

"You saw what I'd been missing right away, didn't you? Why didn't you point it out? Why run the risk I'd go on insisting that Joey was as unreliable a witness as I'd once been?"

"Maybe I should have said something," she'd answered shakily, all too aware of his touch on her mouth and the sudden lack of distance between them. "But I thought there was a bigger risk that you wouldn't be able to move past the pain if you didn't come to terms with it in your own way."

"And that was important to you?" He'd looked disconcerted, and then, as if he'd felt suddenly restless, he had let his hand fall. "I'd better get up to the gate if I'm going. I told Joseph I'd give him a break around midnight."

Guarding the gate, Tess thought now as she let her glance wander casually around the room, taking in the dark-stained wood of the bookcases, the heavy oak table the four of them were sitting at. Del had told her that this was where his teenage charges did their correspondence school assignments during their time at the ranch. Her gaze passed over Connor.

It didn't take a Freudian to see a double meaning in his hasty excuse to leave last night. She had no doubt he'd promised to relieve Joseph Tahe for a while from the young Dineh's sentry duty at the perimeter of the Double B property, but she had the impression that Connor had found it equally imperative to close himself off after his openness with her.

One moment he'd been touching her lips. The next he'd been striding down the drive to where the pickup was parked. He'd been fine with the physical closeness, Tess thought, annoyance flickering through her. If she'd suddenly grabbed the worn leather of his shoulder holster and pulled him down to her mouth, if she'd wrapped one bare leg around his and snugged herself up against the hard length of his body, if she'd let him carry her to the spare bedroom and—

She cut the fantasy off abruptly. The point was that Virgil had been more than comfortable with the physical closeness between them, she thought repressively, wondering if the heat she could feel in her cheeks was visible. But any emotional closeness scared the hell out of him.

Which I already knew, she told herself. Resolutely she focused her attention on Paula as the female agent spoke.

"If Quayle went into that alleyway with the intention of killing MacLeish he must have had a good reason to have wanted to eliminate him. The only one I can think of is the murder of MacLeish's wife ten years ago. Let's say Quayle had some connection with the case back then, never believed in the suicide theory, and thought Mac had gotten away with murder. One day, completely by chance, he sees him alive and well and decides to take it upon himself to dispense the justice MacLeish escaped ten—"

Paula pursed her lips. "Nah, you could drive a truck through that, it's got so many holes in it."

"Maybe a small imported car," Del said with a wry grin. "The way I see it, if Quayle was dirty enough to contemplate murder, he wouldn't have been the type to have been outraged by what he saw as an unpunished crime. And if we're going on the assumption that MacLeish didn't kill his wife in the first place, then that eliminates it as a motive for Quayle."

His gaze rested briefly on Connor. "We are going on that assumption, right? That if Mac's innocent of Quayle's murder he's innocent of Huong's?"

"For now." Connor's voice was steady. "But that leads us to the one question nobody's asked yet. If your old buddy was framed for the murder of his wife, why hasn't he come forward with the truth during the intervening ten years? Hell, if you're right and the suicide scenario was a setup, too—a setup that obviously failed, since MacLeish didn't die in the Rio Grande as everyone thought—why didn't he go to the

authorities as soon as he'd escaped whoever was trying to kill him?''

"Dammit, Connor, I just can't answer that.'' Del
slumped back in his seat. "It couldn't have been that
he was too scared to come forward, because the John
MacLeish I knew didn't scare easy. That's why he
would have been a good senator if he'd had the
chance to run for office. He made no bones about the
fact that he approved of taking a tough stand against
organized crime, and he didn't flinch from naming the
mobsters he intended to go up against. One of them,
Jack Vincenzi, actually threatened legal action. Vincenzi's as crooked as they come,'' he added in disgust, "but he's always protested he's just a legitimate
businessman.''

"Ah, yes, our Jackie,'' Paula said, her tone sour.
She looked at Connor. "He's stayed below the Bureau radar for the past few years, but before you
joined the Albuquerque unit we used to keep a couple
of agents permanently assigned to him. We never
even busted him for a moving violation, although
about six years ago we thought we almost had him.
The case fell through,'' she said with a grimace. "I
wasn't involved, but I remember being told that the
witness refused to testify, or something along those
lines.''

Connor frowned. "If MacLeish was shooting off
his mouth about taking Vincenzi on, then we should
be looking for a possible link between Quayle and
Vincenzi. Between Quayle and Vincenzi and Jansen,'' he amended. "Forget Rick Leroy for the time

being. He's a follower, not a leader, and my guess is he's taking orders from Jansen.''

"Forget Jansen, too.'' Paula shook her head. "Arne Jansen's in the running to head up that national organized crime task force, remember? You can bet if he's ever even stopped Vincenzi in the street to ask him the time he's erased any record of the encounter. We're not going to find—''

"That's it. That's our motive. Jansen and Vincenzi are erasing records.'' Tess heard the hoarse croak in her voice, but normal speech was beyond her. She slid her shaking hands from the table and clenched them tightly in her lap. "Somehow MacLeish can connect the two of them, and they need him dead so Jansen gets the task force position you just mentioned. That's how Jack Vincenzi silences witnesses, Paula—not by paying them to recant or persuading them not to show up at trial, but by killing them. He killed Joy Gaynor.''

Her throat tightened even more. "Or maybe I did.''

Across the table Paula sucked in her breath with an audible hiss. "There was a reporter involved,'' she said slowly. "How could I have forgotten? Joy spilled her story about overhearing Vincenzi order a hit on a judge to an investigative reporter for the *Albuquerque Times*. The reporter convinced her to go to the Feds with the information, even said she'd wait in her own car in the parking lot where the meet was supposed to take place, so Gaynor wouldn't feel so nervous.''

"Joy wasn't nervous,'' Tess said dully, "she was terrified. If it hadn't been for me she never would have been in a warehouse parking lot that night, and she never would have been shot behind the wheel of her car.''

Beside Paula, Connor's gaze widened momentarily. Tess shook her head. ''This isn't an *Eye-Opener* exclusive, Connor. I saw it happen and I recognized the hit man as one of Vincenzi's men. But when I decided that the only way I could make Joy's death less meaningless would be if I wrote the whole story just as she'd told it to me and got my editor to run it on the front page, I was told that the paper had checked out a few vital facts, and my story didn't hold up. Heck, my career didn't hold up after that.''

''A few vital facts like what?'' Del growled.

''Like the hit man had a cast-iron alibi for his whereabouts that night. Like Vincenzi could prove he hadn't been in the city on the day Joy had told me she'd overheard him give the order to kill the judge. Like the judge himself said the whole notion that an upstanding citizen like Mr. Vincenzi would have reason to want him dead was ridiculous. That same judge took an early retirement later that year. Some stocks he'd owned had done exceptionally well, apparently.''

''He was bought off.'' Angrily Del shoved his chair back. ''Seems to me we've got enough to make some kind of a case, Connor. Why can't Paula contact Jansen's superiors and tell them what we've come up with?''

''Because we don't know how high up the tree the rot goes,'' Connor replied sharply. ''Dammit, Del, less than an hour after I made that call to Jansen from the motel, a couple of hired killers showed up to eliminate not only me but Tess and Joey, as well. There's every possibility that if Paula calls the Bureau from here, we'll be signing the death warrants of everyone on the Double B.''

He took a deep breath. When he spoke again his voice was emotionless. "You're our ace in the hole, Paula. Can you get a look at the Albuquerque police file on the investigation into Huong MacLeish's murder without tipping Jansen off?''

"I'm no rookie, Virge," his partner replied. "In fact, I've got a tad more seniority than Arne does. I think I can manage to sneak out a file or two without him learning of it. I'll check into Quayle, too.''

She looked at Hawkins, her normally easy manner returning. "Thanks for the hospitality, Del. Connor tells me you got hitched less than a month ago. If I hadn't heard that, I might have made a play for you myself—and not just because you make the best chili I've ever eaten, although that's definitely a point in your favor.''

She grinned and got to her feet. "But I guess your Greta beat me to the post. Story of my life, darn it.''

Paula Geddes was potentially in more danger than any of them, Tess thought a few minutes later, watching from the verandah as Connor and Del saw the agent to her car. And yet she hadn't allowed that to shadow the good humor and warmth she'd shown during her brief sojourn at the Double B.

"I figured she was dead.''

Startled, she whirled around. Joey was standing beside her, one of Daisy's pups tucked like a football under his arm. He squinted at the dust cloud behind Paula's departing sedan.

"I figured Skinwalker would go for Paula first, then Bill, then Rick. That was before I knew Rick was working with him," he said thoughtfully. "But I knew Paula was the best shot, 'cause once she told me she won a medal for sharpshooting. So when I heard the first body fall in the apartment, I thought it was her. I'm glad it wasn't," he added. "Bill was nice, but Paula used to tell me jokes and bring me comic books."

When I heard the first body fall... What kind of world was it, Tess thought in sudden anger, that those words should *ever* come out of the mouth of a child? What kind of people were Jansen and Vincenzi and Leroy, that they could see children as pawns, as targets, as *victims?*

But she didn't have to ask herself that question, she thought heavily. She knew what kind of people Jansen and his cohorts were. Impulsively she dropped to her knees and gathered a surprised Joey to her in a hug, puppy and all. They would look like normal men. They would help a neighbor jump-start his car battery, barbecue hamburgers in the backyard in the summer, talk about the weather with the mailman.

They would look like regular joes. And some of them would abuse their adopted—

"Hey, Tess, you're squeezing Chorrie." Joey didn't sound concerned, and as he wriggled out of her grasp there was a pleased little grin on his face. He replaced it with a tough-guy scowl immediately.

"Connor said I got to be careful with him. Like not drop him or anything."

"Sorry, sorry." Hastily Tess swallowed the lump in her throat. "I guess I got carried away there, champ." She eyed him with delayed suspicion. "Chorrie? You've named him?"

"After Chorizo, the horse that sent Connor sailing when he was here a long time ago. Connor told me only Gabe ever rode him, but that was because Gabe was part Dineh, and he could ride a dust devil if he wanted." Joey hesitated. "Connor said I shouldn't get too attached to Chorrie, because I might not be able to keep him. *Can* I keep him, Tess?"

Joey had stoically endured far too much in his short life. If he'd fallen in love with a darn puppy, by God she would make sure he got to keep it.

Besides, who was Virgil Connor to tell her nine-year-old nephew to put a wall up between him and his heart's desire just to be on the safe side?

"Yeah, sure you can keep him, if Del says you can have him."

This time it was Joey who squeezed her in an impulsive hug. He released her just as quickly, but she saw pure happiness shine in his eyes.

"Thanks, Tess! I'll walk him and train him and show him how to do tricks and…and *everything,*" he promised. "And he'll be a good guard dog, too, you'll see. I'm gonna go ask Del now."

"Ask me what?"

Del was making his way up the porch steps, Connor a short distance behind him. Hawkins held the screen door open for Joey, and Tess could hear the rumble of the ex-Marine's deeper tones mixing with the high-pitched excitement of Joey's voice as they disappeared into the house.

"You told him he could keep the puppy, didn't you?" Connor reached down and gripped her hand, pulling her upright. "Don't you live in an apartment?"

"Apartments cost rent. Rent means money. Money comes from jobs, and I've probably lost mine by now," Tess said flippantly.

She caught his glance of concern and shrugged. "I'm exaggerating. Good tabloid journalists with a rabid following are hard to come by, and the *Eye-Opener* won't pink-slip me over a couple of missed columns. Heck, the next time Del goes into town I should ask him to pick up the latest issue. I wouldn't be surprised if its front-page story is all about their daring reporter Tess Smith's presumed capture by aliens."

"I heard she was selling used cars with Elvis." Connor's smile seemed forced. "I feel like going for a walk. Want to come?"

"I'd better rescue Del from Joey. This morning one of the Tahe cousins was minding him, and I don't want Del to think I'm using him and his ranch hands as baby-sitters." She shook her head regretfully. "Maybe later."

"No problem." He jammed his hands into the pockets of his jeans, his manner indifferent. He descended the steps, and she stood stock-still, watching him as he headed resolutely toward the horse barn.

"Oh...dear...God." The exclamation came from

her as slowly as if it was being pressed out. She put her hand to her head, her fingers massaging out the sudden crease in her brow.

"You've gone and done it, haven't you?" she said out loud, her tone too low to be heard by anyone but herself. She raised her head and stared disbelievingly at the man striding across the yard. "You've gone and fallen in love with him, for no good reason at all."

No good reason, except that he was a man who found it hard to reach out to other people, and he'd reached out to her yesterday when he'd sensed that Paula's question about the accident had upset her. No good reason, except he'd told her a truth last night he'd never told anyone else, not even himself.

She didn't need reasons, anyway. The deed, Tess thought in defeat as she caught up to Connor at the barn, was done.

"I changed my mind," she said by way of explanation to him as they strolled into the stall-lined enclosure, right now empty of horses. "Besides, you know me—I make a habit of pumping people for personal information. What did Del say as you two were walking back to the house that put you in such a crappy mood?"

And when you've answered that one, I've got a few others for you. Like, how am I supposed to act around you now? Do you think this might just be temporary insanity on my part? Have you ever fallen in love yourself, and if not, do you think you ever could, and if so, do you think you could with me? Would you treat Joey as your own son? Am I going too fast for you?

Have I said any of this out loud?

Her last question was answered first and obliquely by his scowl. "I'm not in a crappy mood. I'm not in a great mood, but I'm not in a crappy mood."

"Okay, then why aren't you in a great mood?" She shrugged. "Aside from the obvious reasons, of course."

"The obvious reasons being that I've had to hide out while my partner rides off into the sunset to try to save my ass, and with every day that passes I wonder if Jansen's unearthed my sealed juvenile file showing my connection to the Double B and figured that I might have brought you and Joey here?"

He exhaled. "Del contacted Jess Crawford. Jess is on his way to the ranch right now, apparently."

"And you wish Del hadn't entrusted Jess with the information that we're here," she said hollowly. "Maybe we'd better leave before he arrives. Too many people as it is know Del took in three reclusive guests a few nights ago, and if your friend gets careless and lets slip the wrong word to—"

"Not trust Jess?" He gave a short laugh. "Hell, I'd trust him with my life. I just don't like him that much. I told you, he and I have always rubbed each other the wrong way."

"I know what you said, but I didn't realize we were talking Hatfield and McCoy dislike," she said dubiously. "Is he really that awful? Why did Del ask him to come, anyway?"

"Because Jess Crawford is Crawford Solutions,"

he grunted. "And no, he's not awful. He's a billionaire, a charmer, and most people think he's an all-round nice guy. But he's a people person."

She shook her head, lost. "The Crawford Solutions reference I get. He's the Jess Crawford who's a computer genius and whose software practically runs the Pentagon, the White House and every law agency in the country?"

Connor nodded. "With his resources, Del's hoping he can help us get whatever information we need on Jansen and Quayle that Paula can't access. And he probably can," he added grudgingly.

"So, what I don't get is the people person—" Tess stopped as Connor put out a warning hand. "What?"

"See that stall?" He nodded at a seemingly unoccupied one just ahead of them. He gave her a grim smile. "That's hell. The devil lives in that stall, or at least he's living in it this week while a cut on his left hind leg heals up."

"That's Chorizo's stall? I'd like to see him."

"He doesn't want to see you. He doesn't want to see me. Chorizo would be happy never to see any human being again in his life, with the occasional exception of Hawkins." Connor reached for her arm to draw her away. "Hawkins horsewhipped the man he found abusing Chorizo as a colt. Quite a feat, since at the time Del was confined to a wheelchair."

A snort came from the stall. It didn't sound friendly. She stepped away from Connor's grasp.

"Don't get too close." He closed the distance between them again. "I wasn't entirely joking about this gelding being the devil. Del says that being confined this week while the other horses are out to pasture has really set him off.''

''I won't get too close,'' she promised. ''I just want to—''

There was a sound of hooves scrambling for purchase on the stall's wooden floor, and then from over the top of the enclosure's latched door a head appeared.

She caught her breath.

He was beautiful. Flared nostrils, the velvety-looking skin around them mottled with an irregular spotting of dark and white, twitched as he drew in the unfamiliar scent of her. His head was less mottled, but still patterned with the same dark on white, and the pale, sparse mane looked almost stubbled. A white ring encircled the liquidly large eye watching her—a characteristic, Tess knew, of a true Appaloosa.

The big animal turned his head slightly. Her awed gaze turned to shock.

''His *cheek*,'' she whispered. ''What happened to him?''

''The son of a bitch Del whipped did that to him with a knife,'' Connor said huskily, his gaze fixed as hers was on the horrific gully of a scar running along the gelding's cheek and just missing his eye. ''He's got other scars, too, but this one's the worst. The veterinarian Del took him to when he found him said it had to have been done when he wasn't much more than a colt. He's got every right to hate people, but that doesn't change the fact that he's—*dammit,* Tess!''

She felt no fear. She'd never felt any fear around

horses, Tess thought, and her trust in them had never been betrayed. The only memory she had of her father was of gentle hands encircling her waist as he set her on a horse much like this one—the Appaloosa he'd raised and trained himself, the Appaloosa he'd been riding in a rodeo earlier on the day he'd been killed.

Warm breath blew from round nostrils. A soft whicker came from the massive throat. Even as Connor grabbed for her, she touched her fingertips to the straight nose.

"Yah-ta-hey, Chorizo," she murmured, using the traditional Dineh greeting. "You and I, we know each other well, don't we? And we've both known monsters."

The gelding whickered again, dipping his big head as if in submission to her touch. Connor took her other arm.

"I've never seen him behave like this with anyone, not even Del," he said quietly. "But let's go now, Tess."

He was silent as they walked back along the length of the barn. It wasn't until they stepped outside that he turned to her with the question she'd known he would ask.

"Where are yours?"

His voice trembled with anger, but the anger, Tess knew, wasn't directed at her. It was directed at a man Connor had never known, a man he would never now know. Shadowed gray eyes held hers as his hands framed her upturned face.

"Where are your scars, sweetheart?" he whispered unevenly. "And how old were you when the monster hurt you?"

Chapter Eleven

She was talking but she still hadn't answered his question, Connor thought ten minutes later as Tess paused in her narrative to smooth at a small rip in the black leatherette of the couch she was sitting on. They were in the office and supply room attached to the barn; a more private location for their talk, he'd decided, than the stable area they'd been in. Private or not, the slim woman sitting in front of him looking down at her hands still hadn't answered the questions he'd asked.

Or maybe she was answering them, he thought as her low tones resumed. He was Belacana, as she'd once said. But Tess Smith was Dineh. If she was to answer his questions at all she would do it in the unhurried way of the People, whose tradition of oral history had been handed down from generation to generation, keeping their past alive.

"My mother's mother died when I wasn't much more than a baby, but I'm sure I remember her. Her own grandmother had survived the Long Walk, and Nali—" Tess's smile didn't erase the darkness behind her gaze ''—Nali is our name for Grandmother— passed on the story to Darla and me.''

Connor blinked, and in the brief instant while his eyes were closed he saw a ragged and endless trail of people stretching out along a black hilltop. He met Tess's slight frown.

''The Long Walk,'' he said huskily. ''When the Navajo's homes were burned, their livestock slaughtered, and they were forced to relocate three hundred miles away.''

''Eight thousand men, women and children,'' she said softly. ''When they were allowed to return home four years later, two thousand had died.''

She sighed and went on, her fingers moving unconsciously in her lap. It was as if she was spinning the thread of her story and then weaving it into a pattern for him to see and understand, Connor thought, resisting the urge to still those restless fingers, to press his own to those moving lips and tell her she didn't have to relive this. She needed to relive it. And she'd chosen him to relive it with.

''So Nali passed on our history to those who would listen. And my mother made it her life's work.'' Amber eyes glanced up at him. ''She was a Dineh storyteller. She spoke in libraries and schools to children, telling them of First Man and First Woman, Coyote and the other animals, the meaning behind the Moccasin Game. She loved what she did, and she was happy that her work allowed her to move from place to place with my father. He was a clown.''

This time her smile was real. ''A rodeo clown, Connor. He distracted the bulls from goring the riders they'd tossed. But his real love was horses.'' She looked down at her lap again. ''He and my mother would have loved the Double B. They hoped to start a breeding ranch themselves one day.''

''When you found Darla's photo in Joey's backpack at the motel, you told me your father had died when you were young.''

It seemed a lifetime ago, Connor thought in faint disconcertion. Had he really only known her for three days? And at that first encounter, had he really been foolish enough to have seen her as a female, and slightly older, version of Joey? The short, boyish haircut revealed the delicately molded line of her jaw, and her T-shirt and jeans followed the curves and dips of what was indisputably a woman's body. He felt sudden heat rise in him, and with an effort forced the inopportune response to subside as she continued.

''He was killed by a bull that was charging the front row of the spectator stands. I was only five years old at the time and Darla was eight, but we were both old enough to know that my mother was devastated by his death. She loved him so much, you see.'' She shook her head, and at the small movement a feathery strand of dark hair curved along her cheekbone. ''But she loved us, too, and that's why she married again a few years later—because she felt we should have a father, and although Brad Turow wasn't Dineh, he seemed like a good man and a good provider. Not eight months after she married him, she caught a cold that turned into a lung infection. It took her life.''

''And you and Darla were left with Turow.'' Connor couldn't hide his anger. "When did he start showing his true colors?"

"Almost right away. He wasn't happy about being saddled with two adopted daughters, and he let us know it. At first he just got stricter—sending Darla to her room for not finishing her homework fast enough, making me go to bed for laughing too loudly at a television show. But then he started using his belt on us. He used it on our backs so the teachers at school wouldn't wonder why it was too painful for us to sit down."

Something flashed behind her gaze. "He's dead. He's been dead for a long time. But I still can't forgive him for what he did to two little girls, Connor. No child should live in fear the way we did. For some reason I seemed to set his anger off more than Darla did, and I know she was terrified that one day his violence toward me would turn murderous."

"You were afraid to tell anyone?" he asked tightly. "Your teachers? Neighbors?"

"We told everyone." Her tone was flat. "And no one believed us."

"But if he used a belt there must have been proof. How could any reasonable person deny that kind of evidence?"

"Proof and reason, Connor?" She looked at him with hard eyes. "Most of the time he was good at leaving no proof. And our stories seemed unreasonable to the people we tried to tell. He was well liked, well respected, a pillar of the community. Most thought he was a saint for putting up with the obviously unbalanced children of the Navajo woman he'd married. In the end Darla found her own way to stop him from beating me.''

A young girl lying stiffly on a bed, her eyes squeezed shut. That same young girl floating above the bed, her mouth wide open in a soundless scream. He didn't know how he'd gained the knowledge of what she was about to tell him, Connor thought sickly, but somehow he had. He'd been balanced on the thin edge of death, and perhaps that had been enough to enable him to see into the soul of the woman whose life force had brought him back.

It didn't matter how he knew. What mattered was that a young girl had been violated in the most heinous way of all.

''He said he'd leave me alone if Darla let him do what he wanted.'' Tess's voice was a dry rasp. ''And so she…she—''

Her eyes squeezed shut. The restless fingers in her lap stilled. The low cry that came from her parted lips seemed to be ripped from the very depths of her soul, and immediately Connor was on his feet, pulling her from the couch.

''Don't say it,'' he commanded unevenly. ''You don't have to tell me any more, sweetheart.''

He didn't want to let her go, he thought fiercely as he tightened his hold around her, felt her tears soaking hotly through his shirt. He *never* wanted to let her go. He wanted to fight the monsters for her the rest of his life, change the endings of her stories, give her back the home that had been taken so brutally from her so long ago.

He wanted all that. Why in the world did wanting all that seem suddenly dangerous?

He frowned and pulled her closer, but even as he did she pushed herself slightly away. Her eyes met his.

"I have to, Connor—don't you see? The ones who are left tell the story. That's how the truth survives."

"I know," he said huskily. "I just can't stand to see you hurting like this."

She smeared away the tears with the back of one hand. "It hurt more all these years to keep it inside. It hurt more to feel ashamed that someone would someday see this."

She moved out of his arms and turned her back to him, at the same time lifting the white cotton of her T-shirt up to her shoulderblades. Pain sliced through him, and for a moment he couldn't speak.

The marks on her back weren't as deep or as wide as those on the maimed Appaloosa, but they bore witness to the same agony and cruelty as Chorizo's prominent scar. The thin white lines criss-crossing the otherwise smooth cinnamon skin would once have been open and bleeding, Connor thought. The physical wounds had healed, but the emotional ones were still visible.

She'd used the word *ashamed*. He could take that away from her, at least. Spreading his hands on either side of Tess's rib cage, he brushed his mouth along the worst of the scars.

He felt the small shock that ran through her. He raised his head, gently pulled her shirt down and turned her to face him.

"Tell me the rest," he said steadily.

Her eyes were wide and dark, her lips slightly parted. She swallowed and gave him a tiny nod.

"He went to Darla's bed every night for two years, and then one night he tried to come to mine. She shot him with his own gun." The quaver that had been in Tess's voice a few sentences ago was replaced by sadness. "She killed the monster before he could get me, and after that night I never saw her again."

"She ran away?"

"Took me to a neighbor's, told the woman to call 911 and then disappeared into the night. She was only seventeen years old. It couldn't have been easy for her, especially after she became a mother a few years later and Joey's father deserted them, but I think if Darla were alive now she would be proud of the way her son turned out."

"Her son and her sister," Connor amended. He tipped her chin up. "We're going to keep the monsters away from Joey, Tess. Even if Paula can't dig up anything on Jansen, I'm hopeful she'll find something in Quayle's background that we can—"

"Del told me I'd probably find you—oops. Sorry, Virge, I should have knocked. Want me to go and come back in again?"

The man sticking his head into the room through the half-open door was of medium height. His features were pleasant, his grin apologetic and his expression as he met Connor's gaze held genuine warmth.

There'd really never been any good reason to dislike him, Connor thought stonily. Not until now. He resisted the urge to slam the door on that billion-dollar grin.

"Don't bother." He turned to Tess, and was caught off balance as he saw the tentative answering smile she was giving the interloper. His introduction came out in a curt growl.

"Tess, meet Jess Crawford. He was sent to the Double B fifteen years ago for hacking into his school's computers—and he's the only one out of the four of us who ended up proving crime really does pay."

"ULTRALIGHTS. I don't know why everyone doesn't zip around in 'em. What a freakin' rush, man." A forkful of sirloin halfway to his mouth, Jess shot a suddenly guilty look across the table at Tess. "Uh-oh, my bad," he muttered. He frowned at a wide-eyed Joey. "You heard 'fudgin',' right? What a *fudgin'* rush."

Joey grinned. "Whatever you say, J-man."

"C-man, dude. *C* as in Crawford. I guess *C* as in Connor, too, but I've always called him Virgil or Virge," Jess added. He gave Connor an innocent glance. "Right, Virge?"

"Except for that time when I convinced you not to," Connor said briefly. "You planning on eating those carrots, Joey, or just fooling around with them?"

"Fooling around with—" Joey caught the glance Tess leveled at him, and changed his answer in mid-sentence. "Eating them," he mumbled, spearing two with his fork.

Tess hid a smile. A steady diet of Jess Crawford would have the same effect on her young nephew as snacking on candy bars for breakfast, lunch and supper, and although she had no trouble dealing with Joey's natural exuberance, she wasn't about to let him cross the line. But from what Jess had said when he'd walked back from the barn a few hours ago with her and Connor, he was only staying the night. Besides, she couldn't really blame Joey for finding Jess's bad-boy behavior amusing.

She did, too. He was outrageous and irrepressibly ridiculous. And after her cathartic outpouring to Connor this afternoon, she felt able to cope with a little ridiculousness.

It had been as if a crushing weight had finally rolled from her shoulders—a weight she'd been carrying for most of her life. Out of all the people in the world who might have taken that burden from her, it had been the man she'd first seen as closed-off and rigidly repressed who'd done it.

Except the way she'd first seen Connor was nothing like the man he really was, she thought. She wouldn't have fallen in love with him if that had been the case. She'd fallen in love with the man she'd glimpsed behind that closed-off wall, the man whose emotions had been plainly written on his face as he'd listened to her, who hadn't been able to hide his anger, his compassion, his—

His *love* for her?

She wasn't sure of that last one, Tess admitted to herself with reluctant honesty. When he'd taken her in his arms, he'd gathered her to him as if he had finally found the woman, the place and the position he'd been searching for all his life, and intended to hold on to what he'd found. But a heartbeat later she'd thought she sensed a hesitation in him.

Maybe that had been her imagination. Maybe everything had been in her imagination. Or maybe she wanted too much from the man, too fast.

Because some part of Virgil Connor would always remain Virgil Connor—slightly boxed in, slightly reserved in certain situations, slightly too serious slightly too often. She accepted that, Tess thought with a slow smile. She'd witnessed at first hand that reserve falling completely apart at least once, and she fully intended to see if she could make it fall apart again when the opportunity presented itself.

Although Jess might beat her to it, if not in the same way. It was obvious Connor felt toward him as Chorizo would about a burr under his saddle, and equally obvious that since Jess had arrived, Connor's hold on his self-control had been slipping.

She wasn't the only one who'd noticed, she realized, as Del lifted one eyebrow in shared amusement with her before turning his attention to his newest guest.

"Last month you were saying everyone should try solar-powered snowboards, this month it's flying around and risking your neck in an ultralight plane. You know what your problem is, Jess?"

Connor grunted audibly, and Del's lips twitched upward. "Too much money, too many toys, no wife. You should start thinking about getting married one of these days."

"Good idea. Who to?" Jess said with ungrammatical promptness. "You finally got smart and scooped up Greta after clinging to your bachelor ways for too long. For about three seconds after I met her last month I thought I might have a chance with Susannah Bird, but then I saw the way she looked at Tye and I knew I wasn't even in the running. Until a few hours ago I thought all the good ones were taken." He looked at Tess, one blue eye closing in a wink. "Now I'm not so sure."

His leer was so absurd that she couldn't prevent a bubble of laughter from escaping her. Laughing at foolishness felt good, Tess realized. Had she ever actually done that before?

"You finished, dude?" The empty plate in front of Joey seemed answer enough for Jess as he grinned at the boy. "I dumped my stuff in the last bedroom upstairs. On the bed you'll find a couple of prototype computer games and a gadget to play them on that hasn't been released on the market yet. Can you try them out and report back to me tomorrow morning on whether they're any good? I think there's a space-battle simulation and some kind of gnome-world-treasure-maze thingy."

"Boy moves fast when he wants," Del observed mildly as Joey, with an awestruck *"Cool!"* took the stairs two at a time, Chorrie as usual tucked under one arm. "Good thinking."

"You made his evening, Jess," Tess said, smiling at him.

"When Del told me on the phone there was a nine-year-old involved I tossed them in my duffel bag."

Tess shrugged. "Hey, I knew we had some serious business to get down to, and I figured Joey didn't need to sit around listening to us talk about what we're up against."

"Between the two of you, looks like you've got Joey's bases covered for this evening," Del observed. "Connor told Billy Tahe to pick out something for Joey when he went into Last Chance this afternoon for supplies. What'd Billy come up with, anyway, Connor?"

"I don't know." Connor rose from the table. "I'm making coffee if anyone wants some."

"What do you mean, you don't know? I saw you take the package upstairs yourself to put it on his bed," Del contradicted.

"Oh, Connor, you didn't have to buy something for him," Tess protested, getting up from the table herself. "But it was nice that you did. When Joey's finished blowing up universes he can go nuts with what you got him." She smiled at him as she started to clear their plates. "Really, what is it?"

"Modelling clay," Jess supplied helpfully as he moved to the sink with his own plate. "Right, Virge? I was chewing the fat with Billy just before supper and he said that's what he got. Five different colors, at that." He shook his head at Tess. "No, sweetie, leave Virge's plate, he's still eating."

She looked down in confusion at the plate in her hand, and then choked back a quick laugh as she saw the lonely slice of carrot still sitting on it. She gave Jess a similar glance to the one she'd given Joey earlier.

"You're bad. I don't envy Del having to ride herd on you fifteen years ago if this is what you're like now." She turned to Connor. "Joey'll love the modelling clay, I'm sure, Connor. Kids don't always feel in the mood for exciting, action-packed..."

She floundered to a halt at his look of patent disbelief. Then she tried again. "I mean, once he's tired of having fun he—" Again she stopped, aware she was making matters worse.

For a moment his expression remained unchanged. Then she saw a spark of wry humor behind those gray eyes. "Well, sure," he said dryly. "That's what I was going for—unexciting and dull. I was a little worried about the five-colors thing, but as long as you make it clear he only gets to use one color at a time I think we can keep him from getting too hyper over it."

Virgil Connor had made a joke, Tess thought as his half smile became a real, if reluctant, grin. Maybe having Jess around wasn't such a bad thing for him, and despite the wickedly mischievous jabs his old buddy kept aiming his way, Jess had dropped everything and come to Connor's aid as soon as Del had contacted him.

The way both Connor and he had done for Tyler Adams not long ago, from what little she knew about the recent problems at the ranch, she mused. Fifteen years ago four hell-raising teens from disparate backgrounds had been forced to serve time at the Double B for crimes ranging from computer hacking to grand theft auto. Who would have guessed that the bond they'd formed then would still be holding firm when they were men in their thirties with responsible careers?

Although *firm* didn't mean it wasn't capable of fraying slightly, she realized an hour later.

"Well, well, what do we have here?"

Jess's laptop was open on the kitchen table in front of him, its digital video interface display—she was pretty sure that was what he'd called it, Tess thought uncertainly—showing the progress of the half-dozen programs he was running at the same time. Images flashed up on the screen and disappeared rapidly, but one progress window had frozen on a photo of a document. Jess looked past her to the screen door, where Del and Connor were talking quietly on the porch outside.

"No, don't call them," he said in an undertone. "My ass would be grass if Virge knew I'd accessed this, and I guess I really should do the right thing and delete it." Absently he made a beckoning gesture with his index finger, and the document immediately expanded to fill the whole screen. "But I just can't resist. Must be the hacker in me."

"What is it?"

The images that had been flashing by were culled from all existing databases in North America, Tess knew—photos caught on security cameras, ATM videos, law enforcement files and every other imaginable source capable of containing even a single frame of film. On Connor's instructions, Jess had commanded one Crawford Solutions program to search for photos showing Jack Vincenzi with either Quayle, Jansen or Leroy. The other five programs had been set with dif-

ferent search parameters that could prove a link between the mobster and the three agents.

When Tess had comprehended the scope of the
searches, she hadn't been able to suppress a slight
sense of revulsion.

"But surely everyone's life isn't on file somewhere, is it? Is *mine?*"

"'Fraid so, sweetie," Jess had replied unrepen-
tantly. "I guess it's possible someone living in the
depths of the Borneo jungle might not be included,
although I wouldn't bet on it. Not with the capabilities
of satellites these days. But don't worry, the hard part
is accessing all this." He'd allowed himself a com-
placent smile. "These programs are light-years ahead
of anything even the CIA or the Pentagon have, and
until I'm sure all the bugs have been ironed out of
them I won't consider releasing them to the government. So, for the next foreseeable while, the only person who gets to snoop on this kind of scale is me."

His smile had disappeared and his tone had taken
on an uncharacteristic seriousness. "It's a power I
don't abuse, Tess. I wouldn't deliberately dig around
in anyone's background for kicks any more than I'd
snoop through my host's personal belongings if I was
a guest in someone's home."

Deliberately had obviously been the key word in
his declaration, Tess realized now as she glanced over
Jess's shoulder at the document filling the screen. Because what he'd stumbled across and was examining
with no apparent qualms was—

"Virge's juvie record. Jeez, I knew our Virgil was
a brawler when he was younger, but I didn't realize

he'd come damn close to making a career of it." Jess
sounded awed. "Eight…no, nine run-ins with the law
before he got bounced up against the judge who gave
him the choice of a year at the Double B or doing
real time. I'm always ragging on him to loosen up a
little, let go of some of that tight-ass control he keeps
himself reined in with, but after looking at this record
I'm just as glad he's never listened to me."

"Jess! You said you didn't abuse these hacker programs," Tess said, appalled. "That's *exactly* what
you're doing. You get rid of that right now, or I'll—"

"No, leave it up, Crawford."

With two strides Connor was at the table, his expression shuttered. His hand clamped around Jess's
wrist as his friend began to make the gesture Tess
knew the computer's action-activated screen would
recognize as a delete command. Planting his other
palm flat on the table's surface, Connor bent over
Jess's shoulder and perused the document on display.

"That one was a bum rap," he muttered, his gaze
flickering over dates and details. "Five guys jumped
me in a parking lot, started kicking the crap out of
me. What's a poor street-fightin' boy to do?"

"Put four of them in the emergency ward with broken bones, leave the fifth one dangling from a street
sign by his belt?" Jess ventured. His grin was lop-
sided. "Dammit, Virge, I know I was out of line. I
should have listened to Tess and—"

"The rest of them were valid charges, from what I
remember." Connor released Jess's wrist and
straightened to his full height. His voice was ice.
"Hell, no, Crawford. I'm the one who should have

listened to you all those times when you told me to let go of my tight-assed control. But better late than never. Let's take this outside.''

"No one's taking anything outside. I didn't stand for it fifteen years ago and I won't stand for it now.'' Del's face was thunderous. He looked at Jess. "Of course, fifteen years ago I'd have put you on KP duty for a month, for pulling a damn-fool stunt like this. What were you thinking?''

"I wasn't,'' Jess admitted honestly. He pushed his chair away from the table. "But that's no excuse, and I know it.'' He looked up at Connor with a ghost of his normal jauntiness. "Land sakes, Mr. Virgil, I thought my card was full, but I do believe I owe you this waltz, don't I? Shall we step outside and take a turn around the dance floor? With you leading, naturally.''

He swallowed, and began to get to his feet. "Don't forget, my nose is my best feature, Vir—'' He stopped, his grin halfhearted. "Connor,'' he corrected himself heavily. "I've got this coming to me, Connor. Let's get it over with.''

"Please don't.'' Swiftly Tess put her hand on Connor's arm. Beneath her fingers she felt muscles like iron cords. "Joey thinks the world of you—of *both* of you. He doesn't need to see any more violence, especially between two men he looks up to.''

Connor held her gaze. Then the hard light behind his eyes faded, and she felt some of the tenseness seep from him.

"You're right, he doesn't. And I don't need to handle my problems this way anymore.'' He jerked his

head at Jess, a certain weariness in the small movement. "Sit down, Crawford. It appears I'm not the
dancer I used to be, luckily for you."

Slowly Jess sank back into his seat, his eyes still
on the man standing over him. Without looking at the
screen in front of him he made a flicking motion with
his wrist as if he was throwing a piece of trash into
a bin. The document vanished.

"I'm a jerk, but not a total jerk, Virgil," he said
quietly. "I know you could make ground-round of me
if you wanted to. I owe you, buddy. One day I hope
I get the chance to pay—"

"What's that?" At Del's query, Tess glanced at
the ex-Marine. He was staring at the monitor. "That
envelope with the exclamation point. Does that mean
anything?"

The varying screens on the display were still blurring through their programs, but now taking center
stage was a depiction of a closed envelope. Even as
Tess watched, she saw the exclamation point on its
flap change to a question mark.

"Probably not," Jess said with a shrug. "That only
indicates that information related to one of the
searches has just come in. Kind of like a running ban-
ner showing late-breaking news at the bottom of your
television screen. But I'll check it out."

He made a movement that Tess didn't see, and the
flap of the envelope opened. As if it were being slid
from it and unfolded, a black-and-white square moved
in front of the envelope and expanded to fill the
screen with an image that she recognized as a rough-

up galley of a newspaper item, accompanied by a photo.

The photo was a head shot of a blandly featured man with thinning blond hair. The lines of type beside his picture were still being filled in, as if they were being composed even while she watched.

That was because they were, she realized a moment later.

"I'll say this is late-breaking," Jess murmured, his attention on the multiplying lines scrolling across the screen and beginning to surround the photo. "Someone in the set-up department at the *Journal* must be downloading this right now. We're watching the morning's newspaper being made, people."

"...concrete-encased body was discovered on the construction site yesterday evening at approximately eight o'clock when a quality-control error necessitated the removal and repouring of a portion of the building's foundation. A site worker claims the body had identification on it in the name of—" Tess stopped reading and blinked. "What's going on now? It's starting to erase. Is that a glitch, Jess?"

"No, that's not a glitch." He looked disconcerted. "That's actually happening. The story's being deleted."

"You mean an editor changed his mind about running the item?" Del frowned.

"I guess." Jess didn't sound certain. "Or maybe—"

"Or maybe an editor was persuaded to change his mind about running it," Connor said tightly. "Strongly persuaded. I'll lay you good money we never hear anything more about this, either in the papers or on the television. It's been buried, just like that body was.''

''But if it was supposed to run in the morning paper and the time given in the article was eight, yesterday evening…'' Tess glanced at the clock on the wall. ''That would mean the body was discovered tonight, right? Just over an hour ago. Are you saying someone moved that fast to kill a story about a dead man?''

''I'm saying Arne Jansen moved that fast,'' Connor said grimly. ''I recognized the photo. The dead man's Rick Leroy.''

Chapter Twelve

She was beginning to make a habit of creeping down-stairs in the middle of the night to the Double B's kitchen, Tess thought, feeling her way past the pine table in the dark and wincing as she stubbed a bare toe on the leg of one of the chairs. If she'd thought of it she would have made this phone call a few hours earlier, just after Connor had dropped his grim bomb-shell on them and with equal grimness had asked Jess if there was any way he could bypass the deletion. When Crawford had shaken his head Connor had shrugged.

"I didn't think so. Dammit, another line or two and we might have found out when that concrete was poured."

"Why is that important?" Del had grimaced at his own question. "Of course. That would tell you when the body was dumped, since it had to have been while the cement was still fresh. We're talking a time frame of what?—five days since Leroy was alive and well enough to kill Danzig and come close to killing Paula at the safe house?"

"The safe house was compromised six nights

ago.'' Connor had rubbed his jaw. ''And once the construction site foreman discovered that, for whatever reason, the cement hadn't set correctly, he wouldn't have wasted more time than he had to in ordering it removed and repoured, so I'm assuming that by today it was hard enough to show flaws. Which means that yesterday it definitely would have been impossible to drop a body into it without leaving a trace.''

''So Leroy was killed sometime between Sunday night and Wednesday night.'' Jess had raised an eyebrow. ''Maybe I'm missing something, but why should we care when the son of a bitch got fitted for a cement overcoat, presumably by his ol' buddy Jansen?''

He'd returned to his usual flippant manner, Tess had noted. As if in reaction, Connor's reply had come out in a growl.

''Because I think inside the box, pal. Because I like to find the logic behind things, and if I don't have all the facts I can't make all the connections. That good enough for you?''

''Sir, yes, sir.'' Jess had rolled his eyes. ''I guess you're going to want to know exactly where this construction site was, too? Just so's you can build your freakin' box nice and tight,'' he'd added under his breath.

''That part I'm not too worried about,'' Connor had said with deceptive mildness. ''If I'm right, the site's—''

''It's visible from the safe house, isn't it?'' Tess had cut in. She'd given him a quick glance of apology. "Sorry. But I just remembered Joey mentioning something about watching dump trucks and cranes from his bedroom window in the apartment building where the Agency was guarding him."

"Less than a block away," Connor had agreed. "Probably not relevant, but like I say, the more facts we have the better."

Not exactly the *Eye-Opener*'s policy, Tess thought as she felt her way to the wall-mounted kitchen phone without doing any further injury to herself. But despite the tabloid's breezy reportage style, more than a few of its scoops on celebrities had proven to be the titillating truth, and those secrets had invariably been ferreted out by the same man.

Unfortunately, that man was invariably drunk by this time of the night, she acknowledged glumly as she dialed his home number. But what did she have to lose? As Jess had explained, his computer programs were useless unless the information was documented somewhere. And all reference to the discovery of Leroy's body had seemingly been wiped, not only from the newspaper's files, but from police records as well.

Besides, drunk or sober, Winston DeWitt could find anything out about anyone—for a price.

"And, dammit, you knew just what his price would be, didn't you?" she muttered out loud an hour later as she finally hung up the phone and massaged her ear, which felt hot and numb after being pressed against a receiver for so long. "Hangar 61, every gruesome detail about that ridiculous alien autopsy, every conspiracy theory about UFOs. The man's certainly got a bee in his bonnet about—''

The rest of her sentence ended in a croak as a shadowy bulk appeared on the other side of the screen door. A stuttering heartbeat later she realized the bulk was Connor.

''Tess? What the hell are you doing up? Why isn't the damn light on?'' He entered the kitchen, closing the door behind him and flicking on the switch that controlled the hanging lamp above the table.

''Using the phone,'' she said in an angry whisper. ''And I didn't put the light on because I thought you were asleep in your room, for heaven's sake. Do you have any *idea* how close you came to giving me a heart attack just now?''

''Using the phone?'' He lowered his voice to match hers. ''Are you crazy? We're hiding out here and you phoned—''

His tone had risen again. He strode past her and impatiently flung open the spare bedroom door. ''Get in, dammit. We need to talk, and I get the feeling I'm not going to be able to keep this down to a whisper.''

''I asked a colleague on the *Eye-Opener* to check into that construction site.'' Tess swept past him into the room. She stopped in front of the small fireplace and turned to face him, her arms crossed over her T-shirt. ''Winston cares who shoplifted what in Hollywood, Connor. He doesn't—''

''You called a reporter.'' Despite his stated reason for transferring their discussion from the kitchen, his words were ominously quiet. ''It was bad enough Del brought Crawford in on this, but what you've just done goes way over the line. Go wake up Joey. We're getting out of here.''

''Do you want to shut up and let me explain?'' He wasn't the only one who could lower the temperature of the room with his tone, Tess noted with some satisfaction. She gave him a glance as cold as her voice had been. ''Winston DeWitt isn't your run-of-the-mill reporter. He's a drunk and a gossipmonger, but he happens to have contacts all over the place. And all he ever wants to know about me is whether I set off airport metal detectors when I walk through them.''

Confusion overlaid his frown. She sighed.

''Hangar 61. When DeWitt's in his cups he's convinced I based it on a real experience. He's as cynical as they come on any other subject under the sun, but he's a UFO nut. He's almost certain I was abducted by aliens at some point and had a microchip implanted in my neck. When I phoned him, I strung him along with some inane excuse about strange lights in the sky over Albuquerque for the past few nights, and told him I thought that concrete had been intended as a landing pad, but that something had gone wrong. I asked him if he could find out when it had been poured and told him he'd probably run into a government cover-up, so to keep it on the QT.''

''He bought that?''

''He was thrilled,'' she retorted. ''And if anyone can get that information for us, it's DeWitt. It was a calculated risk, Connor, but not much of one. You said it yourself this afternoon—it's hard to just sit around doing nothing while Jansen could be getting closer every day to finding us.''

"That's why I'm not going to keep sitting around," he muttered, raking a hand through his hair. "I'll keep my cell on and if you learn anything from your wacko friend, call me. In the note I'm leaving for Del I'll tell him to do the same if Jess ever irons out the damn bugs in his search programs."

"He said he didn't think it was a bug," she argued halfheartedly. "I'm no expert but couldn't he be right? Isn't it possible that Jansen took the precaution of firewalling—" She stopped. "What note? What do you mean I can call you when DeWitt gets back to me? Where are you going?"

"To Albuquerque," he said shortly, turning from her. His gaze lit on a collection of small change on the top of the dresser, and absently he scooped up the coins and dropped them into his jeans pocket. "I won't need a razor," he murmured. "The scruffier I look the easier it'll be to fit in."

"Albuquerque?" She stepped in front of him, blocking his way. "No."

"Tess, I'm in a hurry." He tried to sidestep her. "Billy Tahe's going into the city this morning to deliver some of his sister's turquoise-and-silver work to a gallery there, and Joseph said he'd be stopping at the gate on his way to the highway. I'm going to see if I can catch a ride with him."

She didn't move. A muscle moved in his jaw. "For God's sake," he growled. "Daniel had the right idea. Innocent or guilty, MacLeish is the key to all this and there's a good chance he's hiding out in the area he knows best. If I can hook up with Daniel, that doubles our hopes of finding him."

"*A* plus *B* equals *C*," Tess agreed thinly. "I guess I can understand how you might see that as the logical course of action. Have you considered whether Arne Jansen might be operating on the same logic?"

His mouth tightened as he placed his hands on her shoulders. "Look, Billy wants to be well on his way before dawn. I don't really have the time to justify my reasons right—"

"Dammit, Virgil!" Even as he started to maneuver her aside, Tess grabbed the front of his sweatshirt. She gave it a tug forceful enough that he had to move in to keep his balance.

"Jansen's people aren't looking for Daniel! He's safe enough wandering around asking questions about a man who's got the same tattoo as he does, but you'll be dead before nightfall if you go to Albuquerque, and you know it. 'Armed and dangerous.' 'Take down by any means possible.' Remember those phrases? Jess says he's confident he can get the information we're looking for if you'll only give him time, so—"

"So what?" Connor broke in. "So let Crawford take care of everything? Hell, all he managed to accomplish tonight was to hack his way into my juvenile record, and if he could do that, what's to stop Jansen and his mobster pal Vincenzi from taking it one step further and finding out about the Double B? Maybe you think Jess is the greatest thing since sliced bread, but I can't pin my hopes on him coming up with the answers we need."

"That's really what this is about, isn't it?" She stared at him, taking in the furious heat behind the cool gray of his eyes, the rigidity of his posture. "I don't *believe* this. You're acting like a damn teenager, for God's sake. This has turned into a competition between you and Jess, hasn't it?''

She released her grip on his shirt. ''Maybe the two of you should have had it out, thrown a few punches,'' she said with flat disapproval. ''Maybe that would have gotten whatever problem you have with him out of your system. But I doubt it. It's driving you crazy that you're not in control of this situation, and you're willing to take any insane chance to prove to yourself that you're still handling everything. Well, you're not. Nobody can handle everything and some things can't be controlled, so get used to it.''

''Control?'' His tone was thin. ''Hell, lady, you've got it all wrong. I don't want control, I'd like to let go of it completely. And my problem isn't Crawford, it's *you*.''

''I'm your problem?'' Frustration boiled over in her, and she threw her next words at him like a challenge. ''Then the solution's right under your nose, Virgil. Lose that damned control of yours for once and *deal* with your problem!''

Crystal-gray eyes blinked at her. Then Connor took a deep breath and scrubbed the back of his hand across his mouth. ''It's not that simple,'' he said, starting to turn away.

''It's not that complicated,'' she snapped.

Before he could take a step, her hand was on his biceps and spinning him back to face her. She grabbed his shirt again, pulled him closer, and let go of his arm long enough to wrap hers around his neck.

''For crying out loud, Virgil, you don't have to live

up to your name *all* the time,'' she breathed, bringing his mouth down to hers.

He stiffened. For a second his lips remained unresponsive. Then his hands came suddenly up to cup her face.

''You're probably right,'' he muttered against her mouth.

Without warning, his mouth opened against hers. Tess felt a white-hot heat race through her, electrifying all her senses—no, not electrifying them, she thought disjointedly, more like melting them. Overloading them.

In a moment she wasn't going to be able to pull away, she told herself. If she was going to do it, she had to do it now.

She almost didn't make it. And as Connor lifted his head and directed a slightly unfocused gaze on her, she almost changed her mind.

But not quite.

''Where'd you learn to make love?'' Her voice sounded shaky. She tried to counteract it with a frown. ''Come on, Virgil. Where? From whom?''

His eyes lost their unfocused look. He narrowed them at her, his lashes almost obscuring their gray gleam. ''What is this, twenty questions?''

''No, just one. Where did you learn to make love?''

He shook his head. ''Hell, I can't remember. It was a long time ago, dammit. I was fifteen, she was eightee—''

''You didn't,'' she interrupted. ''You don't know the first thing about it—in fact, you probably think of it as one of those unnecessary frills like putting furniture in your apartment. It was the same when you kissed me at the motel. You're sexy as hell, Virgil, but you come on like gangbusters.''

His gaze widened fractionally before narrowing again. ''So sue me, honey,'' he said with a tight smile. ''I do everything like gangbusters.''

His breath was shallower than normal, and his hands were open at his sides, almost as if he could still feel her skin against his palms. This was what he'd looked like fifteen years ago, Tess thought suddenly. This was how a younger Virgil Connor would have looked—edgy, dangerous, ready for action.

She was pretty sure she could take him on.

''Well, here's a tip,'' she informed him. ''Women like a little soft music, a romantic buildup, maybe some flirting first…but we can live without all that once in a while. What most of us draw the line at is the hundred-watt bulbs overhead.'' She saw the slow grin that lifted a corner of his mouth and felt her own lips curve into a small smile.

''Hit the lights, Virgil,'' she said softly. ''Then let's see if we can slow you down a little.''

Even before she'd finished speaking, his hand had gone to the switch on the wall beside them, leaving the lamp on the bedside table as the room's only illumination. Its subdued glow was just enough to take the shadows from the room, and it was just enough to let her see the gleam of heat in his eyes as he reached for her.

''Slow,'' he said hoarsely. ''I gotta remember that.''

His mouth covered hers, and as Tess's lips parted

she felt the tip of his tongue flick against hers and withdraw. It moved past her lips again, this time deeper, and a ribbon of sensation curled languidly along her spine. She arched her back slightly, moving more completely into his arms.

Without warning, his kiss deepened and his palms moved from her shoulders to slide through the short tendrils of her hair. His tongue teased hers, moved past it, licked against the softness of her inner mouth.

Slowly.

She'd made a big mistake, Tess thought in dazed consternation. She'd remembered why Connor had been sent to the Double B all those years ago, but she hadn't stopped to think about why he'd been so good at being a bad boy. He hadn't walked away a winner from the confrontations of his past by rushing blindly into them—he'd studied his opponents' timing, he'd learned their weaknesses, and then he'd moved in.

He was doing that to her right now. She was *loving* it. Slow heat spilled through her, touching her breasts, sizzling down her thighs, making her gasp.

"Too fast?" Connor murmured against her mouth. "Because I can rein myself in a little more if you—"

"You win." Another trickle of heat ran through her and she bit her lip. "If I cry uncle will you play fair?"

He shook his head, his gaze holding hers. "I lost this fight to you in a run-down dump of a motel four nights ago." He paused, as if rethinking what he'd said. "Hell, I lost it at that diner. I was just too dumb to know what had hit me."

Through the thin material of her T-shirt she felt his

biceps tighten against the side of her breast where his arm was encircling her. He looked at her with sudden uncertainty.

"I want to make love with you, Tess. I know I came on strong a few minutes ago, but I wasn't thinking this was just sex. I don't want you ever to believe that."

He'd used the word *love,* Tess thought slowly. He hadn't said he loved her, hadn't even said he thought he was falling in love with her, but he'd used the word love. A piece of the wall that surrounded Virgil Connor had just fallen away.

And the last of her own doubts had vanished.

"I...I don't," she said unevenly. "I know we both want this, Connor."

As if he'd only been waiting for her acceptance his mouth came down on hers once more, and this time it wasn't too fast, wasn't too slow, wasn't anything less than perfect, Tess thought. At some point her T-shirt came off, and within seconds after it did she'd helped him strip his sweatshirt over his head, both garments falling unheeded to the floor.

Still kissing her, Connor reached around one-handedly to unfasten her bra. Even as his fingers met the tiny hooks, she felt him freeze.

He raised his head and swore softly under his breath. "Dammit, that's the kitchen phone," he muttered. He looked at her, and in the light from the lamp she saw the hard flush of color on his cheekbones, the strong pulse at the side of his throat. "Let it ring," he said huskily.

"We can't." She shook her head, fighting the impulse to go along with his suggestion. "It's going to wake up the whole house, Connor. Maybe not Joey, but Del and Jess. And I don't want them to—I'd rather they didn't—"

He touched her lips. "I get what you're trying to say, honey," he said with a wry grin.

He was out of the room before the third ring, and, stopping only to pull her shirt on, Tess followed him. As quick as she was, as she entered the kitchen, he was already hanging up the receiver. He turned to her, a bemused expression on his face.

"High squeaky voice, called me 'dear boy'?" he asked.

"That would be DeWitt. Correction—that would be DeWitt just prior to passing out. I told you, when he's in this state he loves talking to me about his pet theories. I suppose that's why he phoned back so soon?" Something in his attitude sharpened her attention. "Don't tell me he already had an answer for us."

"A partial answer. You were right, he's good." Connor raised an eyebrow. "Your Winston can't tell us yet the exact time that cement was poured, but according to a worker it happened Sunday afternoon. Apparently the construction company has run into vandalism problems that delayed this job, and they're working weekends and overtime to make the project deadline."

"But Sunday was the night everything happened at the safe house." Disappointment filled her. "Winston's information doesn't narrow it down much more than it already was. I'd hoped to hear Tuesday or

Wednesday, so we'd only have a two- or three-day time frame to deal with.''

"Oh, our time frame got narrower. It's now down to hours, not days,'' he said absently. He caught her frowning glance and came toward her. "Sorry, I'm doing that control thing, aren't I? Plus I wish DeWitt had chosen a more opportune moment to relay his news to us.''

His arm around her shoulders, he steered her in the direction of the bedroom door. "Because of the vandalism, the construction company hired a security guard to watch the site, and because of the deadline, starting Monday a second crew of workers began pulling night shifts. DeWitt's trying to find out when that security guard went on duty Sunday. That's important, because from that point on the site was never left unattended.''

She looked up at him swiftly. "But that means—'' She stopped as the full realization hit her. Connor nodded.

"Yeah. That means Leroy's body was dumped sometime between the time he shot Paula and killed Danzig and the time the guard arrived.'' His smile was tight. "Jansen had him eliminated right after he did his dirty work for him at the safe house.''

Chapter Thirteen

"Funny thing." From his position in front of the cookstove Del glanced over the rim of his coffee mug at Connor and Tess. "All this good, clean country air, and you two city types look plain worn-out. You'd think the pair of you hadn't gotten a wink of sleep all night."

"I don't know about anyone else, but the damn crickets kept me up," Connor said blandly. "How 'bout you, Tess?"

She came close to choking on the mouthful of coffee she'd just swallowed. "Me, too." She didn't meet either his gaze or Del's. "Loud crickets."

"They can be bothersome." Del nodded. "I don't find them a problem when Greta's away, but the moment she's back home the darn things just won't let us sleep at night."

Del Hawkins was as bad as the bad boys whose lives he turned around at the Double B, Tess thought weakly, hoping the burning flush she could feel mounting her cheeks wasn't too obvious. And Connor was no angel, either.

Not that she really had a problem with his misbehavior, she admitted, hiding her face in her coffee cup as she felt the heat in her cheeks intensify. Not right now…and certainly not last night.

After DeWitt's phone call they'd picked up where they'd left off. She'd worried briefly that the news the gossip hound had passed on to them might take first priority in Connor's mind, but any fears on that score had been quickly assuaged. All through the night he'd made it very apparent that she wasn't just a priority with him, but that as far as he was concerned the rest of the universe had ceased to exist for the hours they'd spent in each other's arms.

He'd made love to her three times. He'd driven her out of her mind three times. And she'd done the same for him, she thought in glowing satisfaction. Only minutes after he'd walked her back to her bedroom and had returned to his own room, she'd heard Del going downstairs and heading out to start the dawn chores.

The rancher's next words mirrored her train of thought.

"I usually drive up to the gate of a morning, check in with Joseph to see if there was any excitement during the night," he drawled. Tess was almost certain the double entendre had been accidental, but she kept her mug to her lips, anyway. "He said you'd been thinking of hitching a ride to Albuquerque with Billy this morning, but that you must have changed your mind."

Connor met the older man's keen gaze. "It was a damn fool idea," he conceded.

"Foolish but understandable." Del rubbed the back

of his neck. "You néver were the type to like sitting around." He set his mug on the counter. "I've got to go into town this morning, but while I'm in Last Chance you could do me a favor. It'd get you off the property for a while, at least."

"With you gone that just leaves Jess here as any kind of protection for Tess and Joey." Connor grimaced. "Which means no protection at all. Not that Jess didn't learn to handle a rifle like the rest of us did when we were teens here, but ever since he woke up he's been sitting at the library table in the back room, lost in cyberspace. I appreciate what he's trying to do, Del," he added quietly. "I just wouldn't feel easy asking him to take point duty as well."

"Tess and Joey could go with you. When I went up to the gate this morning I meant to give Joseph some antibiotic for one of his great-grandmother's sheep that has an infected ear, but I forgot. If you could drop the medicine off at Joanna Tahe's clinic she'll get it to Alice. It might be interesting for Joey to get his first look at the Dinetah."

"Interesting for me, too," Tess said with a smile. "Naturally I've visited the Navajo Nation in the past, but I'm not familiar with it. We'd be safe enough there for a few hours, wouldn't we?"

"Safer than most places. Joanna's brother, Matt, is Tribal Police. His force keeps a pretty close eye on strangers coming in and going out." Connor nodded. "I'll give Jess my cell number in case DeWitt phones with any new information, and Paula said not to expect a call from her until tonight at the earliest."

"That's settled, then." She made a face. "As long

as I can roust Joey and get him moving. I've discovered he's a dawdler in the mornings, so I should go upstairs and wake him now.''

''Who's DeWitt?'' Del pushed himself from the counter and glanced at the clock on the wall. ''Fill me in on the way to the barn, Connor. I'll get that antibiotic for you to give to Joanna and then I'd better be on my way. The day's awastin'.''

Not as far as she was concerned, Tess thought happily as she and Connor exchanged quick grins and he followed the ramrod-straight figure of the tough ex-Marine outside. She would be spending the better part of this day with Virgil Connor, and spending it showing him a little of her own world. That wasn't a waste, that was a plus. And it was even more of a plus that Joey would get the chance to see something of his heritage.

But her idea of a perfect day obviously wasn't Jess's, she thought in amusement as she paused in the doorway of the library, the mug of coffee she'd brought for him in her hand. Unaware of her presence, he was humming happily under his breath, his gaze locked on the computer screen in front of him.

''Any luck?'' She crossed the floor to the oak table and set the mug carefully down beside him.

''Thanks. I meant to get up and get some myself an hour ago, but things started happening and I forgot.'' Jess looked up with a rueful grin. ''Guess what? It was a glitch, and not some evil firewall thrown up by our archnemesis Arne Jansen. I felt like a fool when I realized it, but I've fixed the problem now. I expanded our search to include Vincenzi's known employees, but I haven't come across Malden and Petrie yet.''

He glanced back at the monitor, and a frown crossed his face. ''Dammit, it's screwed up again. How did that happen?''

''What?''

Tess leaned over his shoulder and saw the same rapidly changing images as she'd witnessed the previous night. As he had when he'd hacked into Connor's record, Jess had stopped one program and frozen the image on the screen, although it wasn't large enough to identify.

''Oh, when I was doing a couple of dry runs to see if the glitch had been fixed, I threw in Tye's name and mine and a few others, Paula's included. The freakin' program's somehow picked up on those names and mixed them into the search on Vincenzi's employees. Well, Paula's, anyway.''

He made a motion and the image jumped to full screen. ''Harlan Geddes. I'll probably have to weed out Harlan Crawfords and Harlan Adamses, too. That blows big-time.''

Tess gripped the back of his chair, feeling suddenly unsteady. ''That's Petrie. That's one of the hit men who tried to kill us at the motel.''

It was foolish, she knew, but just seeing the man's face sent a shiver down her spine. In the photo— obviously cropped from a larger one and taken at some social function—Petrie was wearing a dinner jacket, and a woman's hand was draped lightly over his shoulder, although the female herself had been cut from the picture. The man she had last seen lying dead on the walkway outside the motel was grinning for the camera and holding up a glass as if in a toast.

I should have switched his shoes, too. Just for a moment the ridiculous notion seemed eminently reasonable. *Joey said their* chindis *would follow us, and he was right.*

"I doubt Petrie was his real name."

Connor's voice behind her drove the shadows away. She cast him a grateful look, and as he came up beside her he caught her hand and gave it an unobtrusive squeeze while Jess told him what had happened.

"But you haven't, right?" Connor's question cut across his too-detailed explanation. "You haven't found any Harlan Crawfords or Harlan Adamses or Hawkins or whatever."

"Well, no," Jess began, but again Connor interrupted.

"Then how can you be sure this bastard's name really wasn't Geddes? It's not that unusual a surname."

"Occam's Razor?" Jess looked unconvinced. "I guess it's possible."

"Who or what is Occam and why does his razor have anything to do with this?" Tess asked, her gaze focused on the photo.

"It's a fancy name for the theory that says if there are two explanations for something, the less complicated one stands a better chance of being right," Connor said dryly. "I'm surprised the C-Man knows it. I'm less surprised he didn't call it what everyone else does—KISS. Keep it simple, stupid,'' he added to Jess in a growl.

"I just throw those obscure phrases around to impress you, old buddy," Jess grinned.

"So this razor theory says it's more likely the program's working fine, and it's just coincidence one of Vincenzi's hit men had the same name as Paula?" Tess said thinly. "I think we can make it simpler yet. Jess, can you enlarge the photo more? It doesn't matter if you lose some of his face, so long as you keep his shoulders in."

She felt rather than saw Connor's sharp glance, but she didn't take her attention away from the monitor. As Jess complied with her request she leaned forward and pointed a trembling hand at the image. Even at such a moment she'd remembered her Dineh heritage enough not to point with her finger, Tess thought disjointedly. Some of the inherited strictures were as much a part of her as—

"That braided gold bracelet—see it there, on the woman's wrist draped over his shoulder?" she said shakily. "That's Paula's bangle. That's Paula's wrist."

"Which means..." Jess's sentence trailed off. Connor finished it for him.

"Which means that's Paula's ex-husband, Harlan Geddes," he said savagely. "Also known as the late Agent Petrie."

"I WAS THE FOOL who led her straight to the Double B, complete with giving her directions for getting there." Connor struck the heel of his hand on the steering wheel of Greta's sporty red four-by-four. "I'll never forgive myself for that."

Tess glanced behind him at Joey sitting in the extended cab's back seat. He was engrossed in one of the games Jess had given him, but she kept her voice low just the same.

"She's your partner and you trusted her. *I* trusted her."

"Because she made sure we did, with that phone call to me just after the attempted hit on us at the motel." He wrenched the wheel to avoid a rut in the hard-baked road. "She had to have been there. She must have been watching from somewhere close by just to make sure everything went as it was supposed to, and when she realized it hadn't, she needed to salvage what she could from the situation, fast. She needed us to leave before the real agents Jansen was sending arrived."

A muscle jumped in his jaw. "She played me all the way down the line," he said tightly. "Right up to and including suspecting my own area director."

"But how did she trace us to the motel that night?" Tess answered her own question. "The busboy at the diner. He either phoned the local police and talked to someone who was in the pay of Vincenzi or, if he did get through to the Agency, relayed his message to a dirty agent."

"Or it's Occam's Razor again. When she discharged herself from the hospital, what would have been more natural than to ask which route her partner had been assigned to search, and head out to join up with me? If she'd walked into that diner and flashed her ID minutes after we left, the busboy would have spilled his story directly to her, and after contacting Vincenzi and telling him to start putting the arrangements for a hit in motion, she caught up to us on the highway and tailed us.'' He swore softly. "We saw it all clearly enough, but we were looking at it through a mirror. Paula tilted that mirror just enough so that it showed us Jansen's reflection and not hers.''

"Except for one thing.'' Tess shook her head. "The wound she sustained during the safe house hit on Danzig. Bill must have gotten that shot off when he realized she and Leroy intended to kill him and then go after Joey, but how could Paula have counted on—''

"Bill's gun hadn't been fired,'' he contradicted her. "He didn't even get the opportunity to unholster it, which makes it unlikely that Leroy was an innocent in all this, as well as Danzig. Since he's dead now, too, that possibility had occurred to me.''

Tess stared at him. "You're saying she stood there and let Rick point a gun at her head to avert any suspicion that she'd been working with him, trusting that he'd aim it in exactly the right place to inflict nothing worse than a scalp wound? I don't buy that, Connor. Whatever else she lied about, there was no love lost between her and Leroy. And if it did happen that way, who killed him and dumped his body?''

"Vincenzi himself? One of his paid killers?'' His shoulders lifted in frustration. "We don't have to dot all our *i*s and cross all our *t*s right now. The one thing we can't argue with is the link between her and Vincenzi. Divorced or not, it's obvious she still moved in her husband's circle.''

"Or maybe it was just as much her circle as his," she amended thoughtfully. "Paula didn't do all this as a favor to her ex-husband's boss, Connor. She had a vested interest in having MacLeish killed, and when that went wrong, trying to silence Joey. She had to have had mob connections as far back as when MacLeish was considering running for office on his clean-up platform, and she could well have been involved in the murder of Huong and the attempt to make it look as though Mac had committed suicide.''

"And just like at the motel, she was hidden in that alleyway, watching to make sure Dean Quayle carried out the murder assignment she'd given him?" His gaze narrowed. "She was the third person Joey sensed there that day. She was Skinwalker. She couldn't assume he wouldn't one day recall some detail that would point the finger at her.''

Tess opened her mouth and then closed it again. He was right, she thought. They didn't have time to argue every detail, and at the present moment the topic of Skinwalker was a distraction they could ill afford. She glanced sideways at him, taking in the grim set of his lips, the tense grip of his hands on the steering wheel.

Last night there hadn't been one inch of her skin those hands hadn't stroked, one curve of her body they hadn't explored. Those lips had brought her to ecstasy time and time again, and in turn had cried out her name when he'd followed her over that same ecstatic edge of desire.

And after each shudderingly intense climax had sated them, after the last tiny explosion of sensation had left her those three times, he'd held her in his arms, stroking her hair and wrapping one leanly muscled leg around hers as if he needed to keep her as close to him as he possibly could.

He hadn't said he loved her. But in every small and tender gesture, he'd shown her what he wasn't yet ready to put into words. She'd harbored the hope that their time together today would have taken him a step nearer to tearing down the defenses he'd erected long ago, defenses he no longer needed.

But their time together today would more likely be devoted to contacting Arne Jansen and persuading the area director to listen to what Connor had to tell him, she thought worriedly.

"You can bet Paula's been more than helpful in planting suspicions of me in Jansen's mind, the same way she did with us about him," Connor had said to her and Jess at the ranch. "And let's face it, I set myself up as the perfect patsy by cutting all communication with the Agency four days ago and disappearing with a federal witness and an unknown woman. Even the two dead bodies at the motel make it look like I'm an out-of-control killer, since Paula would have been sure to remove any phony ID before the authorities arrived. I don't want to be on the phone presenting my case when it's possible she's on her way here right now with a few of Vincenzi's hired guns."

"She's cool, all right," Jess had agreed, his normal good humor nowhere in evidence. "It took nerve to

show up here yesterday, listen to the case you presented against Jansen—a case she knew that with a
minimal amount of digging would be proven to be
evidence against her, not him—and then make the
decision to drive off and get reinforcements, rather
than risk taking you and Del on by herself.''

"Nerve?" Tess had known her tone was thick with
revulsion, but revulsion was what she'd felt. "It took
more than nerve to befriend a child, knowing all the
while she intended to sanction his death. At some
point Joey's going to have to learn the truth about
her. What's that going to do to him?''

"Shake his faith in people," Connor had said quietly. "But you'll be beside him to restore it.''

As if he hadn't been able to help himself, he'd
reached out and cupped one palm lightly on the side
of her face, his touch warm. For a moment he'd kept
it there, his gaze holding hers, and then with reluctance he'd turned back to Jess.

"We need to get Joey away from here as fast as
possible, and the Dinetah still seems our safest haven
for now. Paula's never met you, and even if she does
show up she's got no idea we suspect her.''

"I get you." Jess had nodded. "I'll fill Del in on
the situation when he comes back from Last Chance.
Better yet, I'll phone a couple of businesses in town
and leave a message for him to call me. He said something about stopping at the feed store, so I'll try to
catch him there. If the lady shows, I play the dumb
visitor who don't know nuttin' about nuttin'.''

"It'll be a stretch, but do your best." A corner of
Connor's mouth had lifted. Lightly he'd punched his

friend's shoulder. "That thing last night. Water under the bridge, agreed?"

"Agreed." Jess's smile had held a touch of relief. "You guys be careful out there. Tell Joey I'll look after Chorrie for him till he gets back."

Except it wasn't likely Joey would return to the Double B anytime soon, Tess thought as the red four-by-four pulled off the dusty road and into a graveled parking lot in front of a small, square white building. Once Jansen was persuaded that Connor was to be believed, a phalanx of agents would sweep down upon Joanna Tahe's clinic here and whisk the nine-year-old back into protective custody, but with one important difference from the last time he'd been in their care: this time she was going to be with him. If she had to call in the whole of the Navajo Nation to back her up, she vowed, she wasn't going to let her nephew be separated from her again.

"Ever," she murmured out loud. Beside her, Connor shot her a quizzical glance. "A private conversation with myself," she said with an attempt at a smile. "What's the plan?"

"The plan is I use the phone in Joanna's office. Like I said, this conversation's going to take a while, so you and Joey might want to wait inside the clinic while I'm talking with Jansen." He frowned. "I'd have liked more privacy, but on the Dinetah, cell phones are pretty much useless."

He was right, Tess knew. Aside from the atmospherics created by Mount Taylor, transmission towers were few and far between here in the Four Corners region. But Virgil Connor had a lot to learn about nine-year-olds if he thought Joey would be content to sit in a roomful of babies and their mamas, especially when he was already staring out the four-by-four's window at the game of hide-and-seek taking place in the field beside the clinic. The participants were children his age, Tess saw as she alighted from the truck, and likely the siblings of the babies inside, sent out to play while their mothers waited to be examined by Joanna.

She had a few things to learn about nine-year-olds, too, she told herself wryly twenty minutes later. When Connor had disappeared into the clinic and she'd asked her nephew if he wanted her to accompany him over to the group of hide-and-go-seekers, he'd looked at her in consternation.

"They'll think I'm a big loser if I have to have my aunt with me, Tess. I'll be okay, I promise."

And he was, she thought with a small smile, watching him running for the boulder by the side of the clinic that seemed to have been designated home base, and getting there a step ahead of the youngster who was "it" in this round of the game.

Tough little Dineh you raised, Darla, she thought, blinking against the sudden tears prickling at the back of her eyelids. *But how could he not be? Whoever his father was, his mom was the bravest woman I ever knew. I'm going to make sure your son understands that when he's older, but for now it's enough that he's finally come home—that we've finally come home.*

It did feel like home to her, she realized in faint surprise. In this big country that some might see as frighteningly vast and in places inhospitable, she'd felt more at peace with herself than she ever had in the city. Maybe it was the fact that she'd come to know Connor here, maybe it had something to do with the way Del had welcomed her and Joey, but she had the feeling there was more to it than that.

This is the Four Corners. The four sacred mountains stand sentinel around me—Tsisnaajini, Doko'oosliid, Debe'ntsaaa and Tsoodzil. Of course I feel at home here. I am home.

"And so is Connor, whether he realizes it or not," she murmured, a smile playing around the corners of her lips as her gaze idly searched the group of children scattered around the boulder for Joey's familiar grin. "I wonder if he'd ever consider leaving the Agency and joining Del and Tyler Adams in running the Double—"

She couldn't see him. Her gaze sharpened and darted from child to child, quickly rechecking. A boy ran out from behind the whitewashed clinic and she released the breath that had caught in her lungs, but as she exhaled she saw he wasn't Joey.

It was a game of hide-and-seek. He had to be hiding, naturally, and when his aunt came tearing across the parking lot his cherished tough-guy facade would be badly dented. Even as one part of her mind was arguing with the other, Tess sprang into action.

Gravel spurted up from her sneakers as she ran across the parking lot to the boulder just past it, and with an effort she slowed her pace as she approached. "Hello, little sister." She stopped a few feet away from a girl with ribbon-tied braids halfway down her back.

"Hello, auntie." Despite her respectful greeting, the child looked properly cautious. Tess fixed a smile on her face.

"The little boy who was playing with you—the stranger. He's my nephew. Do you know where he is?"

Her explanation seemed to reassure the girl, but she shook her head. The boy whom Tess had seen running from the back of the clinic pulled a face.

"The city boy? He's over there, still hiding." In a typically Dineh gesture, instead of pointing he pushed out his lips in the direction of a small gully behind the building. "I told him we never go there, but he said he wasn't afraid."

"Thank you." She was going to give Joey a tongue lashing he'd never forget when she found him, Tess thought shakily. Or maybe she would really make him sorry he'd thrown such a scare into her—maybe she'd just gather him up in her arms and give him a hug in front of all his new friends.

"That'll do it," she muttered as she jogged toward the gully. "Especially if that little pigtailed girl's watching."

But Joey's dire punishment was going to have to wait. Although the gully was deeper and broader than she'd realized, it was still shallow enough that she should have been able to see him, even with the brushy mesquite growth that provided a thick and spiny tangle at one end of the depression. And he wasn't there.

"Joey!" She tried to keep the fear from her voice as she shouted his name. She didn't entirely succeed. *"Joey!"*

"I…I'm over here, Tess. In the trailer."

Weak relief washed over her and, following it, confusion. Trailer? About to call out again, she glimpsed a sparkle of metal glinting from the depths of the mesquite brush, and saw the barely visible trail leading toward it.

"Here I come, ready or not," she said, her tone crisp. The mesquite-lined path ended abruptly in front of a rusted-out travel trailer, probably once used as someone's high-country summer hogan before being towed here and abandoned. "You know, buddy, I'm a little disappointed in you, taking off like this. You should have realized I'd worry. Get out of that trailer and let's get back to the truck in case Connor's looking for us."

As she spoke she stepped onto the crumbling cinderblock that served as a step up to the abode. The door was ajar, and she opened it fully and stuck her head in.

The trailer was little more than a shell, its interior gloomily dim in contrast with the bright sunlight outside. She could just make out the figure of Joey huddled against the far wall, his legs drawn up to his chest and his gaze not meeting hers.

"No more games," she said impatiently. "It's time to go."

"I…I can't, Tess." His voice was a whisper. "I can't get past *it*."

As the child on the playground had done, he

twitched his lips. Following his fixed gaze, Tess saw nothing but the stained carpeting that covered the floor of the trailer.

"Past wha—"

The words died in her throat as her eyes adjusted to the dimness and she saw the coiled rattlesnake between her and Joey.

Chapter Fourteen

"Joey, don't move." The command came from Tess's dry throat in a croak. "Even if you think it's coming toward you, stay very, very still."

"Tess, get me out of here."

There was fear but not panic in his voice. That was good, she thought. Now all she had to do was work on her own impulse to give in to hysteria.

"I will, champ. I just have to figure out how," she replied, steadying her nerves enough to assess the situation.

It was a diamondback and a big one, probably six—no, closer to seven, she revised as the thing shifted slightly—feet long. Brownish gray, its back was patterned with the darker diamonds that gave it its name, each one outlined with lighter-colored scales. The muscular body tapered to a rattle-banded tail ending in a blunt, buttonlike tip.

Moving as slowly as she could, Tess stepped into the trailer. The snake swung its head around toward her. Its pupils, elliptical like a cat's, seemed to expand, and cold terror washed through her.

She pushed the terror back and studied it, barely daring to breathe.

Its head was larger than its neck, and spade-shaped. Diagonal black lines traveled from those eyes to its jaws, above twin depressions on each side.

She knew enough about rattlers to guess what those depressions were—facial pits, capable of sensing the heat of any warm-blooded body, even one as small as a mouse. In effect, they were sophisticated infrared detectors, Tess told herself fearfully, and right now they were transmitting to the creature a wealth of information about her.

It swung its head away. She let out a cautious breath, and let her own gaze search the floor around her feet.

There was a tumble of tin cans by the door, a rotted scrap of curtain material, and the broken-off end of a broomstick. The stick was little more than a stub, and totally useless for what she had in mind, since she'd heard somewhere that rattlers could strike up to half the length of their bodies. If so, then this one had a strike zone of around three to four feet, and a two-foot length of wood wouldn't serve as a goad to lure it toward the open door while staying out of range herself.

There was nothing to do but find something outside. Backing toward the entrance, Tess looked at her nephew and willed herself to ignore the coiled menace between him and herself.

"Joey, I need something to—"

Behind her something slammed. Instinctively she whirled around.

The door had closed. She crossed toward it with more speed than caution, and turned the knob. It fell off in her hand.

"Tess, watch out!"

At Joey's cry she jerked her gaze back to the diamondback. It unwrapped another coil and extended itself toward her, its head stiffly up. For an endless moment she stood frozen against the door, before it shifted its attention from her.

It slithered lazily from the center of the trailer to one side, and again arranged itself into coils, this time against the wall. Now her sight line to Joey was unimpeded.

In the ceiling above him was a skylight—a square of frosted plastic, propped ajar with two thin aluminum struts. It was large enough for an adult to squeeze through, and certainly large enough for a nine-year-old's body. It was a way out.

"I'm going to come over to your side and boost you up to that skylight, okay?"

Even as she spoke Tess inched her way to the wall across from her, and started sliding slowly along it. At rough estimate, the trailer itself was only nine feet from side to side. That didn't leave much room, she told herself faintly.

"Okay." Out of the corner of her eye she saw him watching her. "That door didn't blow closed, did it, Tess?"

"I don't think so, champ." He knew as well as she did that the day outside was windless and still, so there was no point in lying to him. "I think one of the kids you were playing with shut us in here as a joke, and when he or she saw that the knob was broken they probably got scared and ran off.''

She wasn't entirely sure she believed her own theory. It was obvious Joey didn't, from his next words.

''Skinwalker shut us in.'' His reply held no hesitation, but only hopeless acceptance. ''I guess he wants you, too, now.''

''Well, he's not going to get either of us.'' She was directly opposite the snake, and it was as well aware of that fact as she was. Under her T-shirt her body felt slick with sweat. ''Don't talk anymore, Joey. This is the tricky—''

Like oil ribboning through water, the diamondback smoothly uncoiled and began gliding toward her. Pure adrenaline shot through Tess and she shot sideways out of its path. It stopped in its original position, right in the middle of the floor, and she practically fell onto Joey.

Her heart smashing against her ribs, she grabbed him and gave him the hug he had coming to him. He didn't seem to be taking it as a punishment, she noted light-headedly as two skinny little-boy arms wrapped around her and hugged her back. A rush of love swept fiercely through her, and for a second she squeezed her eyes tightly shut.

She opened her eyes and released him. She tipped his chin up with a lightly closed fist, and met his wide gaze.

''You're going to get onto my shoulders and grab the edge of that opening, okay? Then I want you to hoist yourself through it. When you're on top of the trailer, start shouting for Connor, but try not to move around too much. I...I don't want you to slip and fall off, and I don't think Mr. Snake here likes banging and shaking.''

She saw the urgent question in his eyes, and shook her head before he could speak. "I'm just tall enough to get you out, champ, but I can't reach it myself. I'll stay here and wait for Connor. Now, up on my shoulders.''

The rattler hadn't moved since it had returned to its position in the center of the trailer. As Joey clambered onto her back and Tess straightened to her full height, she saw it watching them with lazy alertness, its forked tongue flickering in and out. She grasped her nephew's ankles.

"Okay, stand up now. Can you reach the skylight?''

It seemed an eternity before he answered. She felt him fighting for balance, and tried to keep her own legs braced as firmly against the floor as possible.

"Tess?'' His trembling voice came from above her head. "It...it's still too high. Let go of my feet and I'll jump for it.''

"No!'' The word came out more sharply than she'd intended. "Stand right where you are and let me—''

"Hello! Anybody in there?''

From outside came a muffled female voice. Tess heard the sound of the mesquite bushes scraping against the metal skin of the trailer, and light footsteps drawing nearer.

"We're in the trailer and the door's broken! I'm trying to get out onto the roof!'' Joey's yell was directed at the open skylight. "There's a snake in here with us, so don't shake the trailer or he'll get mad."

She had to be one of the mothers from the clinic. Tess raised her own voice.

"Please bring help. My nephew's right, there's a rattler here. Tell Virgil Connor at the clinic to come right away."

"No time for that."

There was the sound of a foot stepping cautiously onto the roof, and Tess remembered suddenly that the gully had risen up against one side of the trailer. Whoever their savior was, she'd simply climbed the bank of the gully and jumped onto the roof. Metal creaked overhead.

"If there's one thing I hate, it's a snake. Come on, Joey, grab my hands. You okay down there, Tess?"

This time the voice floated clearly through the open skylight. Tess looked upward in shock, and saw Paula Geddes looking down at her. The female agent grasped Joey's wrists, the gold bracelet on her left arm glinting in the gloom.

"One, two, three—up!"

Joey's feet left her shoulders. Belatedly she made a frantic grab for them, but his legs, kicking for purchase against the lip of the skylight, were already out of her reach. He disappeared and she heard the thump of his body as he fell out onto the flat roof of the trailer.

And then she heard the rattle.

Wrenching her gaze from the skylight, Tess realized the snake was no longer where it had been. The rattle came again, like a burst of percussion, and she saw the diamond-patterned body move slowly along the wall she was standing against.

"Tess, don't move."

Paula's horrified tones came from just above her. Suddenly Geddes was no longer the most immediate threat.

"Don't worry, I won't," she replied. "There's nowhere I could go anyway. I'm too short to reach the ceiling."

Restlessly the snake slithered a few feet away again. Tess eased her cramped muscles and carefully raised her head.

Paula's face was no longer above her. Instead, her body, clad in the same navy pantsuit as yesterday, was already halfway through the opening.

A moment later she dropped lightly onto the floor.

"You're a shortie-pants, all right." She grinned. "I think I'll be able to get myself out after we hoist you through."

"You mean—" Tess shook her head. "It's too dangerous, Paula. That thing's getting antsy, and as tall as you are, you're going to have to jump for that opening. If anything's certain to rouse him to strike, that will."

"We don't have a choice." Navy-blue shoulders lifted in a shrug. "Like a fool, I left my gun locked in my car. When I met Del in Last Chance and he told me you and Connor had taken Joey to the Dinetah, I was thinking a nice, relaxing day, not blowing the head off a rattler. Move it, lady."

Was it possible they'd made a terrible mistake? Tess wondered slowly. Could there be an innocent explanation for Paula's connection to Vincenzi's hit man? Could the hand in the picture of the gunman have belonged to some other woman?

She got Joey to safety. She's risking her life to do the same for me. If she was behind all these killings, it would have been easy for her to throw something through the skylight and goad that rattlesnake into taking care of us for her.

"I...I'm moving." Tess placed her foot into Paula's clasped hands, and shot her a smile. "Sorry," she said softly.

"For what?" Paula grinned. Not waiting for a reply, she grunted in effort and stood a little straighter as Tess gained her balance. "Hurry up, Smith," she ground out. "Can't...can't keep this up for long."

But already Tess's fingers were grasping the skylight's edge. She pulled herself up to a standing position and found her head and torso fitting easily through the opening. With a grunt of her own, she boosted herself onto the trailer's roof.

From her vantage point she could see Joey running across the field to the clinic. She looked into the trailer.

"One good jump and I think I can reach it." Paula's upturned face looked unconcerned, but her eyes were shadowed. Her glance darted toward the snake and then back as she bent her knees and gave a small, flexing bounce. "Here goes noth—"

This time the rattling sound was explosively loud. Even as Paula launched herself upward, the diamondback, moving with incredible speed, obliterated the distance between it and her. In a blur of angry motion its head hurled itself toward her, mouth wide open, knifelike fangs plunging into Paula's calf just as her fingers locked onto the edge of the skylight.

Paula's eyes widened in shock and pain. Her neck arched backward. Her mouth opened in a scream and her grip slipped.

Tess grabbed for her wrist, but then saw the big hand that had suddenly clamped around it. She scrambled out of the way as beside her, Connor hauled a limp Paula through the opening.

"You didn't get bitten, did you?" Fear made his gaze brilliant, but as she shook her head, the fear was replaced by concern.

"Did you see it get her?" he asked tersely, squatting beside Geddes's seemingly unconscious body. He gathered the navy-clad figure into his arms and stood.

"Once for sure." Tess ran ahead of him along the trailer's flat roof and stepped across the small gap between it and the side of the gully. "Connor, she saved our lives. She got Joey out and then she deliberately got into the trailer with that snake to save me. I...I think—"

"I think so, too," he replied grimly. "We made a mistake somewhere, but we'll figure it out later. Run ahead of me to the clinic. Tell Joanna to get the extractor and the antivenom ready. I don't think that bite was dry, but with any luck it didn't deposit a full dose of venom into her."

"It wasn't dry." Paula's eyelids fluttered open. "I'm not in the habit of fainting just to get swept up into a manly embrace, Virge. Something's in me, but it doesn't feel as bad as it could.''

"Shut up, Geddes." His growl was accompanied by an uneven grin. ''Just lie there and let me get you to Joanna Tahe.''

"And here I was hoping you'd suck it out."

As Paula's weak riposte left her lips, her eyelids drifted down again, but by then Tess was sprinting across the field to the clinic.

"THE PROGRAM DIDN'T make a mistake. Petrie's real name was Harlan Geddes, and I found another photo." Back at the Double B, Jess shook his head. "The woman with Harlan in the second photo's definitely Paula—younger, but unmistakably the woman you carried in a while ago and took upstairs to rest, Connor. I don't get it, either. From what Tess told me and Del, she didn't hesitate to risk her own life today to save them."

Of that there was no doubt, Tess thought, remembering Joanna Tahe's verdict a few hours earlier at the clinic:

"The extractor pulled out venom, Connor." She'd glanced at Tess. "It works on a vacuum principle, sucking the poison back through the fang punctures," she'd explained. "Your friend's guess was right, she didn't receive a full dose, but I gave her an antivenom shot just to be on the safe side. I don't think she'll suffer any tissue damage, which can be a major concern with diamondbacks, and she'll probably be back on her feet tomorrow morning. But I don't like the notion of a rattlesnake taking up residence so close to where my patients's children play. Would you take care of it, Connor?''

He'd nodded curtly and had left the room.

''You're Dineh, too, so I know you'd prefer to live and let live,'' Joanna had admitted. ''But it's just too risky in this case. I'll get some men to break into the trailer and remove the carcass, and later on in the week I'll insist that piece of junk gets towed from the property. It's pretty clear another child closed that door on the two of you for a joke, but it could easily have ended in tragedy.''

She'd hesitated. Then, as if performing a duty she had no enthusiasm for, she'd spoken again, her tone reluctantly low. ''Did Connor tell you I have a great-grandmother?''

''Alice Tahe?'' Tess had nodded. ''Del's spoken about her. I'd like to meet her one day.''

Joanna had lifted one eyebrow ruefully. ''You might think differently after I pass on her message to you. My cousins refused to, but I find it hard to say no to Nali.'' Slight embarrassment crossed her calm features. ''Nali says to tell you that you saw what you thought you did on the road that night. She says he wants the boy. Does that make any sense?''

Presumably she'd answered Joanna, Tess thought now, although for the life of her she couldn't remember her response. Connor had come back in and transported a groggy Paula into the back seat of the four-by-four. When they'd returned to the Double B Jess had been about to jump into his own vehicle and come after them. Del had admitted in a phone call that the he'd inadvertently told Paula where to find them.

"It's lucky you didn't get through to Jansen," Del said to Connor.

His rumbling tones broke through Tess's preoccupation. Setting her disquiet over Alice Tahe's message aside for the time being, she looked up as he went on.

"If by some chance the Geddes woman's involvement in this can be explained away, then it stands to reason you were right the first time, and Jansen's the one behind everything."

"Don't think I haven't thanked God and the storm playing havoc with the telephone wires around Gallup for that one," Connor answered tightly. "Joanna warned me she'd had trouble making calls earlier. I must have tried at least six times to get through to the Albuquerque field office, and once I thought I had a connection, but then the line went dead again. By the time Joey raced in and told me what was happening at the trailer, I was ready to heave the phone through a window."

He rubbed his jaw wearily. "Hell, if I could only come right out and ask Paula about those damned photos. After what she did today, I'd like more than anything to trust her again, but this link between her and Harlan just can't be—"

"What's my no-good ex gone and done now?"

Tess's startled gaze flew to the library doorway. Paula, bundled in a plaid robe of Del's to counteract the chilled reaction she'd suffered from the venom, took a step into the room and then stopped. Dark eyes widened briefly as she took in the four of them sitting at the library table.

Connor was the first to recover.

"We were just saying he must have been a fool to let a woman like you slip out of his life," he lied, swiftly getting up and striding toward her. "Dammit, Paula, you look like death warmed over. What the hell are you doing out of bed?"

"Walking into a discussion I wasn't supposed to hear, obviously." Paula shook off his hand. "I still feel a little shaky, but my wits weren't affected, Connor. I've never told you Harlan's name, so your little excuse just now doesn't fool me. You've been digging into my personal life, haven't you?"

"Not yours." Tess shrugged at Connor's slight frown. "We were digging into Petrie's life, Paula. We found these."

Earlier Jess had printed the two photos of Harlan Geddes from the computer's screen. As Paula sat in the chair vacated by Connor, Tess slid the pictures across the table to her.

"Petrie? He's one of the killers from the motel, right?" Paula glanced down at the photos. "Harlan with a glass in his hand. Probably a pair of dice in his pocket, as well, since I don't look terribly thrilled with him in this shot." She shoved the pictures aside. "I don't get the connection."

"What's not to get?" Jess's drawl was edged. "We haven't been introduced, but I'm the guy who found these photos of you and Petrie—sorry, Harlan. Maybe it was the fact your ex had a couple of different names that confused you, huh?"

"A couple of different—"

Paula stopped. Her gaze went to the pictures she'd thrust aside, and beneath the plaid robe Tess saw her shoulders slump.

"I always knew he'd come to a bad end," she said tonelessly. "I didn't think it would be this bad. Harlan was one of the hit men who tried to kill you at the motel?"

"You didn't know?" Connor's question was sharp, but Tess saw fugitive hope flicker behind his eyes. "For God's sake, Paula, are you seriously trying to tell us you didn't have a clue your ex-husband was on Jack Vincenzi's payroll?"

Paula shook her head. "I swear I didn't. I don't expect you to believe me, but it's true. That marriage was the worst mistake of my life, and when I finally got free of that jerk I didn't ever want to see or hear from him again. It wasn't just the memories, either. I'd been accepted into the Agency, and I wanted to sever all connections to the part-time thug I'd been foolish enough to marry when I was a teenager."

Slim fingers massaged her temples. "I rose in my career. It appears Harlan progressed in his, too, if he was carrying out hits for Vincenzi. I'm not sorry he's dead, Connor, I'm just sorry this has come between us."

She stood with an obvious effort. "Not that I've been much help to you on the case. I haven't been able to dig up a speck of dirt on Arne. The man's squeaky clean, although Quayle wasn't, for what it's worth." She shrugged. "He took early retirement from the Bureau only because it was either that or an investigation into some deals he was suspected of making with Vincenzi. There wasn't any documented proof, but it's clear the powers that be were convinced he wasn't someone they wanted carrying a badge.''

She turned to Tess, and for a moment a faint smile touched her features. ''You give that tough Dineh nephew of yours a hug from me, okay? And take one for yourself, lady. I'm glad we got to know each other, even for a little while.''

''Paula, wait.'' Tess was on her feet and at the other woman's side before Geddes could take a step. ''I'm glad we got to know each other, too. And I believe what you say about not knowing Harlan was working for Vincenzi,'' she added firmly. She glanced at Connor. ''I do,'' she said stubbornly. ''I don't think I'd be standing here right now if it weren't for Paula, and Joey probably wouldn't be outside on the porch playing with Chorrie if she hadn't saved him.''

A corner of Connor's mouth lifted. ''You're preaching to the converted, honey.''

He didn't seem to realize the endearment had slipped out, but Tess felt a little flush of pleasure as Paula gave her a quickly surprised look and then a small grin. Oblivious to their unspoken exchange, Connor looked toward the table.

''Del? Jess?''

''Anyone who deliberately takes on a diamondback to save a little boy and a friend is all right in my book,'' Del said gruffly. ''I'm sorry we had the wrong idea about—''

He broke off as the sound of a ringing phone came down the hall. ''No, I'll answer it,'' he said to Connor. "You get things straight with your partner, here."

"Jess, how about you?" As Del exited the room, Connor directed the question to his friend. Jess frowned, and then his usual grin flashed out.

"I guess I can understand you not keeping up with the guy, Paula," he conceded. "Lord knows I've scratched some names out of my little black book that I hope never to run into again."

He shuddered theatrically, and as Paula sat down beside him with a dryly humorous reply, Tess met Connor's gaze.

He hadn't let go of her hand during the drive back to the ranch from the Dinetah. Wedged between them, Joey had cast suspicious glances at both Connor and his aunt, and finally he'd spoken, his tough pose back again after his recent scare.

"You guys in love or something?" It had sounded as if he was asking them if they'd contracted the plague, but Tess had seen the tiny spark of joy at the back of his scornful eyes. She'd felt herself flush and had left the answer up to Connor.

"Or something," he'd agreed easily, giving her hand a squeeze. "You got a problem with that, buddy?"

Joey had thought for a second. "I guess not," he'd said finally. "Hey, Connor, what're they gonna do with that ol' snake's skin? Can I get some boots made from it?"

Or something. Not exactly the balcony scene from *Romeo and Juliet,* Tess thought now in amused exasperation. But she'd come to understand that with

Connor, actions always spoke louder than words. The raw fear in his eyes when he'd thought she'd been a victim of the diamondback, the tight grip of his hand around hers, the way he'd held her last night…

Virgil Connor was in love with her. Now all she had to do was get him to admit that simple fact—to himself and to her.

"I don't know about anyone else, but I'm about ready for supper." Jess grinned up at them. "It's not exactly ranch grub, but I got Del to pick up some frozen pizzas today when he hit the grocery store. How about if I mosey along out to the old chuck-wagon and rustle you wranglers up some chow?"

"Go ahead, cookie. But it's still your turn to do the dishes, so don't think you've pulled a fast one by offering to make supper." Del's sarcastic tone was replaced with an uncharacteristic hint of excitement as he came toward them.

"That was Daniel on the phone," he said, tanned cheeks creasing in a smile. "Son of a gun found Mac-Leish, just like he said he would." He exhaled, obviously savoring the moment.

"Mac's had amnesia for the past ten years. His memory just came back a week ago, after Quayle tried to kill him."

Chapter Fifteen

"So we just sit tight until tomorrow?"

Perched on the verandah railing and staring out into the gathering dusk while she relaxed with Connor, Tess saw Joey's small figure running across the yard toward the wiry frame of Joseph Tahe. The hired hand stopped, patiently bending down to the boy while Joey said something to him.

"That's when Del's friend gets back from those high-level talks he's been attending in Europe." Connor was sitting on the steps. Taking a page from Daniel's book, he was whittling at a chunk of wood. He looked up at her. "Bill Strauss is one of the few people who doesn't have to ask twice to get in to see the president, anytime of the day or night. We need someone with that kind of pull to make sure no fatal accidents occur before we get the chance to present our case against Jansen."

"I suppose we can't take the risk that Vincenzi's influence extends higher than a mere area director," Tess agreed. "You don't really think it does, do you?"

"No, but as you say, best not to take the risk, es-

pecially when we're so close to clearing Mac's name
and nailing Jansen and by extension, Quayle.'' He
frowned. ''I can't blame Daniel for not getting Mac's
story from him yet, especially when the man was in
such poor shape when he found him this afternoon.
He hadn't eaten for days, apparently, and his wound
was infected. But it would have been nice to have had
our suspicions about those two definitely confirmed.''

''They will be,'' Tess said. ''The links Jess's programs found this evening between Vincenzi, Quayle
and Jansen show those three were associated with
each other as far back as ten years ago, at least. And
it couldn't have been coincidence that Quayle's late
brother was the first cop on the scene of Huong's
murder. It had to be the way we guessed, Connor,
Vincenzi wanted MacLeish not only out of commis-
sion but discredited. He had his two dirty Agency
buddies kill Mac's wife and plant evidence to make
it look like he'd done it, and then they were to kill
Mac himself in a faked-up suicide leap off a bridge.''

''Except they were dealing with a man who'd survived five years in a tiger cage, and had been a Double B operative, to boot.'' Connor's smile was tight.
''They picked the wrong Vietnam vet to frame, that's
for sure. I wonder how they found out he was still
alive and living on the streets in Albuquerque?''

''That might be something else Mac can tell us
when he gets here tomorrow.'' Tess squinted into the
dusk. ''What in the world is that boy doing? He's
racing around like a chicken with its head cut off.''

''Chorrie's missing.'' Connor smiled. ''But so are
Daisy and the rest of the pups. Del told me she has

a habit of moving her litters when they're old enough to follow her. He suspects she's found a snug little nest somewhere in one of the barns, but he hasn't come across it yet.''

''Well, Joey isn't going to find Chorrie now, and it's time for him to come in and get ready for bed.'' Tess jumped lightly from the railing. Joseph was shaking his head at his young interrogator, obviously indicating that he hadn't seen the missing pup, either. ''I'll go out early tomorrow morning with him and we'll turn the ranch upside down together.''

''I'll help you.'' Connor stood, too, pocketing the small knife. He followed her worried gaze to a disconsolate-looking Joey, who was now looking in one of the pickup trucks. ''I hope for his sake we find the dog, Tess. From the start I worried that he was getting too attached to him.''

About to head for the yard and Joey, Tess stopped and stared at him. ''I hope nothing's happened to his pup, either, Connor. But if by some terrible misadventure it had, I'd wait a decent while, get Joey another one, and hope and pray he opened his heart enough again to fall in love with it just as much.''

''I know you would.'' He shrugged. ''And you'd probably pick the first one he showed any interest in. Me, I'd at least want him to choose one old enough to have gotten over all the expected puppy ailments, and maybe a dog that had already been trained not to wander away every time he took his eyes off it. Even then I wouldn't be happy seeing him build his whole life around it, the way he's been doing with Chorrie.''

''See, that's just another example of Virgil Connor

wanting everything reasonable and logical.'' She mustered a teasing smile, slightly disconcerted at the turn the conversation had taken and wanting to lighten it a little. ''Love has its own logic, but it doesn't have anything to do with reason or caution.''

She gathered her courage. ''Come to that, who knows why you and I got together? It sure wasn't logical—I'm the wacko who writes for a tabloid and you're the epitome of the just-the-facts-ma'am FBI agent, not just in your work but in your personal life. But we did, didn't we?''

That was as far as she dared go, she thought. She'd given Agent Connor the perfect opening if he had something he wanted to say to her, but he would have to take it from here.

Agent Connor wasn't going to take it anywhere, she realized a heartbeat later as Connor remained silent. In fact, Agent Connor looked as if he wished this conversation had never begun.

She scrambled for something to say that would ease the tension that had somehow suddenly sprung up between them. She'd pushed him too far and too fast, Tess chastised herself. She knew the kind of man he was, and yet she'd practically asked him to declare himself to her before he was ready.

''Anyway, enough about puppies and love, although speaking of puppy love, I think the reason Joey hid in that trailer today was to impress a cute little girl with braids.'' She rushed on, still embarrassed. ''And I forgot to tell you, Connor—he believes Skinwalker locked us in. Alice Tahe does, too, from what Joanna told me at the clinic.''

"What do you believe?" His eyes were unreadable, but at least he was talking again, Tess thought.

"I don't know," she admitted slowly. "I guess I think it's possible, however crazy you must think that sounds."

"Even though your only so-called proof is a little boy and an old lady who says she sees ghosts?"

"And a Dineh reporter," she reminded him. "Don't forget what I saw on the road the night of the accident."

"A split-second vision of something running into the path of your car just as a tire blew," he agreed. "See, to me that's no proof at all. I'd want to look into Skinwalker's eyes, give a tug on that wolfskin to see if it came off. But you're ready to believe wholeheartedly in something you can't prove. I might envy you that ability sometimes, Tess...but that's not me. Do you understand?"

He wasn't talking about Skinwalker. He'd phrased it so that he might have been talking about a dozen different things, but he was talking about himself and her.

She did understand, Tess thought hollowly. She just needed to make absolutely sure.

"Where do you see us going, Connor? You and me, I mean." She felt no embarrassment at all this time, she realized. This was too important to feel embarrassed about. "We made love last night. I think I've got the right to ask."

"I think you do, too." Crystal-gray eyes met hers. "I see us getting to know each other better. I see us going out, spending as much time together as we both feel comfortable with, and yes, making love again. I guess what I'm saying is I see us seeing how it goes and taking it from there."

"Gathering proof?" She stared wonderingly at him. "That's what you're looking for, isn't it? Proof that there's really love between us."

She hadn't expected valentines and bouquets of flowers from a man like Virgil Connor, she told herself. She'd known he wasn't the kind to come up with wildly romantic gestures, passionate speeches. All she'd wanted was that walled-off heart of his, but she'd wanted it given freely and wholly.

He couldn't give her that. Which meant he really couldn't give her anything at all, Tess thought, pain lancing swiftly through her.

Because I don't want to be the logical conclusion you come to. I don't want what we have between us to be weighed and measured and evaluated before you decide the risk factor is acceptably low and you choose to commit yourself. Don't you see that if you were really in love, you wouldn't have a choice…just the way I didn't have a choice about loving you.

Just the way I don't have a choice about what I have to do now, she told Connor silently, her suddenly-blurred gaze still fixed on his face.

"Do you know what I see, Virgil?" she asked him hoarsely. "I see that you don't see anything at all. And I see that it's over between you and me."

"I THOUGHT LIFE in the country was supposed to be peaceful." Paula pushed open the screen door, swatting at a moth that had come into the kitchen with her. "Actually, my little stroll around the barns *was* pretty peaceful until the menfolk started roaring out of the yard in trucks. What gives?"

She smiled at Tess, but Tess didn't feel like smiling back. She hadn't felt like smiling since her disastrous conversation with Connor a few hours earlier, she thought drearily, and yet it had seemed that she'd been forced to keep one pasted on her face almost nonstop.

She had the feeling that when she was ready to talk about things, Connor's partner would be a sympathetic listener, but right now the pain was too fresh. She made the corners of her lips turn up.

"Joseph Tahe contacted Del on the walkie-talkie to report some trouble with the horses in the far corral, since when something like this happens, Del checks into it himself so the gate doesn't get left unguarded. He asked Connor to ride shotgun, in case it was a wolf. As for Jess, he's in the library working on the computer."

"Snakes. Wolves. Worst of all, moths." Paula pulled a face. "I'd rather go up against bad guys anyday."

"Is that why you joined the Agency?" She'd wanted to be alone, Tess thought, but maybe it was better to take her mind off her unhappiness by chatting with Paula. Despite the difference in their ages, the female agent's blunt good humor made her easy to converse with.

"I joined the Agency because I thought I could make a difference. I guess I have, but not as much of one as I wanted." The navy pantsuit had been ruined by the afternoon's encounter with the rattler. Under a sweatshirt of Del's Paula's shoulders lifted. "I don't know if I ran into a glass ceiling or what, but a few promotions passed me by. Now I'm wondering whether our boy Arne had anything to do with that."

"He's killed to protect his career. Stalling a colleague's progress wouldn't be morally indefensible to him," Tess said dryly. "In fact, with him gone you might even have—"

She stopped and tipped her head to one side. "Did you hear that?"

"Hear what?" At the counter Paula hefted the coffeepot hopefully, and set it back down. "Empty. Darn."

"I thought I heard something scratching on the porch."

Tess rose and went to the screen door. Flicking on the verandah light, she looked down as the scratching came again, this time accompanied by a plaintive whimper.

"Chorrie!" Opening the door, she gathered the puppy into her arms, almost losing him as he tried to cover her face with doggy kisses. "Joey's been worried sick about you!"

"Let me guess—you're going to march him upstairs and plop him on Joey's bed, right?" Paula observed with a grin.

"Of course." It was the first real smile she'd felt like giving in hours, Tess thought. She was pretty certain Joey's would be bigger when he woke up to find Chorrie snuggled beside him. "I'll be back in a few minutes."

It had been more of a struggle than usual to persuade her nephew to go to bed tonight. Her promise to help him mount a full-scale search in the morning hadn't gone far to ease his agitation over his missing puppy, and Tess had been sure she'd seen tearstains streaking his sleeping face when she'd gone in to check on him a couple of hours ago.

She pushed open his bedroom door gently. Enough illumination was shafting through the raised window from the full moon outside to see the huddled figure of his body under the covers, and carefully she set Chorrie down beside him. The pup nosed under the covers, pounced on something and presented it to her, his tiny tail wagging.

It was Joey's medicine bag. Firmly she pried the soft leather from Chorrie's gums, and then grabbed at the rawhide thong to save it from being chewed as well. A few golden grains of pollen escaped and drifted to the sheets.

The puppy jumped from the bed and trotted to the door, whining disconsolately.

"Chorrie, come back here!" She hissed the command out in a whisper. When the animal didn't obey she gave up with a sigh. Slinging the medicine bag's thong around her neck, she put a light hand on the blanket-covered hump. "Joey? Joey, wake up. There's someone here to see—"

The hump was suspiciously soft. She pulled the covers back.

The next moment she was racing down the stairs to the kitchen, Chorrie tucked under her arm. Setting the dog on the floor, she sped past a startled Paula to the counter.

"Do you have any idea how this thing works?" she asked tersely. She stared in frustration at the array of unmarked buttons on the walkie-talkie as Paula moved to her side.

"I can probably figure it out. What's the matter?"

"Joey's gone." She slapped the gadget into Paula's palm. "Call Joseph at the gate. Tell him to notify Connor and Del to get back here right away. I'll be out searching the barns."

"You're sure he's nowhere in the house?"

"He's not in any of the other bedrooms, and if he'd come downstairs he would have walked right past me. His bedroom window was open. He had to have climbed onto the porch roof and then down the tree beside the house." Tess turned toward the door. "Tell Connor to hurry, Paula."

"Don't worry, I—"

Beside Paula the telephone rang shrilly. Tess's gaze flew to the other woman's in sudden hope, and swiftly she lifted the receiver from the cradle.

"Hello?"

"You're the aunt, right?" The voice on the other end of the line was brusque. She gripped the receiver more tightly.

"I'm Joey's aunt, yes. Have you found him? Who's this?"

"I've found him. I'll make sure you never do, Ms. Smith, if you don't follow my directions to the letter. Do you still need to ask my name?"

Tess froze. From somewhere a long way away she

seemed to hear her own voice rasping out a reply to his question. "No. You're Arne Jansen, aren't you?"

Beside her she saw Paula stiffen.

"Area Director Jansen," he corrected curtly. "And if you know that, you know that you and Virgil Connor have caused me quite a bit of trouble over the past few days. Here's what I propose."

The man talked as if he were doing nothing more sinister than addressing a Monday-morning briefing, Tess thought sickly. Jansen's very lack of emotion was more terrifying than if he'd been ranting at her.

"I'm willing to hand your nephew over in exchange for Connor. Joey's released unharmed, you get to walk away, and Connor, along with the threat he poses to me, is eliminated. I know Agent Connor. He'll see his death as a reasonable sacrifice in the line of duty, if it means the child lives."

Her mouth felt so dry she could hardly reply. "I don't believe you'd let him and me go free and be content with Connor."

"That's because you're not in our line of work. Put Connor on the line. He'll understand why I'm making this deal."

"He…he's out in the barn." Jansen's deal seemed to hinge on Connor's presence, Tess thought frantically. She wasn't about to tell the man she had no idea where he was right at this moment. She heard him give a sharply impatient exhalation.

"For God's sake. Listen—Joey's no longer a threat to me, and neither are you. From the beginning the boy insisted he saw some kind of boogey-man in the alleyway where that bungler Quayle was killed. I thought he'd seen me. I still think he saw me, but after reading the reports of his conversations with the agents while they were guarding him, it seems he's spinning wild stories about ghosts and wolves. Even if he ever does point the finger at me, he's no longer believable—just as you haven't been since the Joy Gaynor incident.''

''I still don't trust you,'' Tess said woodenly. ''Connor's not the only credible witness against you. Since you've tracked us to the ranch, you're obviously aware that Del Hawkins and Daniel Bird have been working on this investigation alongside him, and unless you're planning to kill them, too, Connor's death wouldn't help you.''

He didn't know Paula was allied with them, she thought. He didn't seem to know about Jess. She didn't need to give him information he didn't have, and that included the fact that Daniel had found John MacLeish.

''The fabled Double Bs.'' There was a dismissive note in his voice. ''Rag-tag survivors of a force that was disbanded after one of their number turned killer in the jungles of Vietnam. Daniel Bird's a convicted felon who's just been released after serving a murder sentence. Hawkins never made a secret of the fact that he thinks MacLeish was innocent of the murder of his wife ten years ago. He'll come off as a zealot who'll accept any alternative rather than break faith with a former brother in arms. No, Connor's the only one I have to worry about.''

He took an audible breath. ''Do I tell you where

you and Agent Connor meet me, or do I hang up the phone right now?''

''Don't hang up!'' Tess swayed against the counter. ''Tell me where we're to meet you. Connor and I will be there.''

His instructions were given clearly and crisply, as if he were winding up the same Monday-morning briefing he'd seemed to be conducting all along. It couldn't be coincidence that the area he'd chosen for the hostage handover was the very stretch of road where she'd had the accident, Tess thought as she hung up the phone. Somehow Jansen had known about the incident.

But he didn't know about Paula. And that was going to be his undoing.

''He's got Joey and he's willing to give him up in exchange for Connor,'' she said, holding up a palm to forestall the urgent questions she could see in Paula's eyes. ''We've barely got time to make it to the handover point, and we certainly don't have time to find Connor. That doesn't matter.''

''Of *course* it matters! As soon as he sees you've come alone, he'll probably kill you and Joey!'' Paula's features tightened in alarm. ''What were you thinking, Tess?''

''I was thinking that I'll get you to ride shotgun with me, just like Connor's doing for Hawkins right now,'' Tess answered, grabbing the four-by-four's keys from a hook near the door.

''Except you'll be hiding out of sight on the floor— and you won't show yourself until you hear a signal from me telling you that you've got a clear shot at Jansen.''

Chapter Sixteen

All in all, a lousy evening, Connor thought as he pushed open the screen door and entered the kitchen. Having to put down an animal was never a pleasant task, but the mare had been too badly savaged to deem it anything but a mercy to put her out of her suffering. They hadn't caught the wolf that had done it.

Del and he had gotten into an argument on the way back here, and Joey's pup was still missing, and none of those mattered a damn compared to what had passed between him and Tess earlier.

She'd given him his walking papers. There'd been some small relief in having the moment over, although it was the same kind of relief a man might feel after days of apprehensive waiting for medical tests to come back and finally being told he was going to die. Del hadn't understood the analogy at all.

"You told the woman *what?*" he'd exclaimed, hand shifting the truck's gears down as they jolted across the field to join up with the road leading back to the ranch.

"I told her we should see how it went before making any big promises to each other,'' he'd replied. ''Dammit, you did the same with Greta. You went out with her for years before you finally popped the question.''

''And I came this close to losing the woman I loved because of my pigheadedness,'' Del had retorted. ''Every time's she's away like this I get an inkling of what my life would have been like without her, and I'm tellin' you, boy, I break out in a cold sweat. I've already made up my mind that when she comes home tomorrow I'm going to tell her that from now on when she needs to attend a showing I'm going with her.''

''What about during the months your bad boys are here?'' Connor had given the older man a wry smile. ''I know you, Del. You won't ever shut down that part of the ranch's operations.''

''I don't intend to. Tye can take it over, and I'll get someone to run the Appaloosa end of the business. Maybe you.''

''Ain't gonna happen. I've got a job already.'' His reply had been prompt—too prompt, he'd realized as Del had peered sideways at him.

''A job you've outgrown—or might have, if you hadn't blown it with Tess tonight. I always thought I helped you out some, that year you spent at the Double B, but I knew you had a long way to go before you became the man you could be. Tess was making you that man, Virgil. You were beginning to open up. I guess that scared the hell out of you, so you put the kibosh on it as fast as you could.''

Del had it all wrong, Connor thought as he passed

through the kitchen and along the hall to the library. He hadn't been scared, he'd wanted to be prudent. It would have been easy for him to have told her what he'd known she wanted him to say; easier yet to hear the same words from her. And if somewhere down the line, maybe not right away, maybe not in the first month, maybe not even in the first year, but at some time, they'd found out it wasn't working, then just the fact that those words had once been spoken would—

Would tear your heart apart. Would shatter your world. It's bad enough now, losing her when you never really had her, but it's a damn sight better than losing her later, isn't it? And you were afraid you would lose her one day. You'd convinced yourself you would, and you'd seen what losing love did to the man you worshiped when you were his son. Del's right. You were too damned scared to take what she was offering you.

He stopped stock-still in the hall. Was it true? Had he really just made the biggest mistake of his life because he hadn't been able to believe in something he couldn't touch, couldn't see, couldn't *prove*—but something that had been all around him nonetheless?

"The womenfolk back inside the house, too?" Jess came out of the library, Chorrie in his arms.

Connor blinked at him. "What?"

"Tess told me she and Paula were going Skin-walker hunting, and asked me to watch the dog for her. I figured that meant they were scaring themselves silly telling Navajo ghost stories and drinking white wine on the porch. They're not?" Jess looked confused. "Then where's Joey? The mutt peed on the carpet, but when I took him upstairs, Joey wasn't there. I assumed he'd woken up and wandered outside to be with Tess."

"When that billionaire playboy gets back I'm going to tear a strip off—" Del's angry growl broke off as he came up behind Connor and saw Jess in the library doorway. "You're here. Then who took Greta's four-by-four out for a spin?"

"I think Tess and Paula did," Connor said grimly. He grasped Jess's arm and marched him back into the library. "What exactly did Tess say when she told you they were going out? How did she sound? Upset?"

"I don't know, I was working on the computer, for heaven's sake." Jess shook his hand off. "Dammit, Connor, you know what I'm like when I get into it. The house could be falling down around me and I'd hardly notice. Although I did hear the phone ringing just before she came in to tell me she was leaving," he added dubiously. "Or maybe that was the call that came just after she'd gone. I actually took a message, so don't go telling me I don't do anything for you, dear boy."

"Dear boy? Winston phoned? She went to meet Winston?"

It didn't make sense, Connor thought worriedly. Of course, with Jess, it often didn't. He took a deep breath.

"What was Winston's message?"

"That the security guard had gone on duty that night at eleven sharp," Jess answered patly.

"Eleven?" Del was still wearing his cowboy straw. He pushed it back, scratching his forehead. "That can't be right."

"That's what the man said. Eleven." Jess looked annoyed. "Hell, if the two of you think I'm so incompetent I can't remember a simple number, here's the proof." He fished in the pocket of his jeans and pulled out a scrap of paper. "I wrote it down. See— eleven. Like eleven bells, eleven lords a'leaping or whatever the fu—"

"Like *News at Eleven*," Connor said slowly. "Like Paula telling us Rick Leroy was ogling *News at Eleven*'s blond anchor babe while she was playing cards with Bill that night in the safe house. Except that by eleven when that guard went on duty, Leroy was past the point of ogling anyone. He was already dead, and his body had been dumped in the newly poured concrete at that construction site."

"But why would Paula lie about a thing like that?" Jess's brow furrowed. "Jansen's the bad guy here, isn't he?"

"Yeah, Jansen's the bad guy," Connor said tightly. "Except he's not the only bad guy. Geddes has been in this with him all along—and right now she's taking Tess straight to him."

"Tess!" Joey tried to run toward her, but Arne Jansen's grip on his collar jerked him back. Under a renegade swath of black hair, dark eyes glared up at the area director. "I *told* you she'd come for me," he said defiantly.

"And you told me you'd be coming with Connor."

Ignoring the small boy he was restraining, Jansen directed his words at Tess. "You lied. The deal's off."

With his sandy, thinning hair and his slightly paunchy figure, the middle-aged man in front of her gave no outward physical clue of the terrible crimes he'd committed, Tess thought, her mind racing. He started to turn back to his vehicle, an unmarked sedan similar to the one that had rolled down this very gully a week ago.

She needed to stall Jansen. During the drive here Paula had warned her she probably would, had guessed the director's first reaction would be exactly what it had just been. With the rough terrain and the glaring headlights washing the scene in dazzling and distorting light, even for a crack markswoman these wouldn't be optimal conditions for a take-down, and they needed Joey completely out of the line of fire before Paula would risk a shot.

She was waiting in the four-by-four right now, scrunched down on the floor in front of the passenger seat. The window on that side was open, and she was only waiting for Tess's shouted signal before she rose up and took aim at Jansen.

Skinwalker was the signal, Tess thought edgily. She wished now she'd chosen something else.

And she wished Connor was here with her.

Arne Jansen might believe that he would have had no trouble eliminating Connor if he'd shown up, but her money would be on Connor, she realized. Somehow he would have found a way to save Joey and defeat the area director. But her and Paula's plan could work, too.

Except she had to stall Jansen right now, or their plan would fall apart.

"Of course I lied to you," she said, sharply enough so that he turned back to face her, Joey still in front of him. "I was afraid you'd change your mind if I told you he wasn't at the ranch when you called. But I left a note telling him where I'd gone and what you wanted. All you have to do is wait for him to show up and then we can make the handover."

For a moment she thought she'd convinced him. Then he shook his head. "Smells like a trap. Maybe it isn't, but I can't risk it. You had your chance, bitch. You blew it."

"*Nobody* talks to my aunt like that!" Joey twisted angrily in Jansen's grasp and aimed a sneaker-clad foot at his knee. "Nobody, do you hear, you big... you big *turkey!*"

"Joey, don't!" Tess raced forward as Jansen's open palm connected with the boy's ear. Joey slipped sideways on the uneven gravel, and fell to the ground, obviously dazed.

It was the best chance they were going to have, she thought urgently. As Jansen made a quickly impatient gesture with his gun hand to keep her back, she raised her voice in a scream.

"*Skinwalker!*"

"You don't have to shout, I'm right behind you. Hi, Arne. Kid got you a good one, didn't he?"

Tess whirled around. Paula grinned at her.

"Yeah, you had it right the first time. Or was me being the villain your second theory? Arne, where do you want to do this?"

"You're working with him? You were on his side all along?" Nausea rose in Tess's throat. She forced it back along with her questions, a higher priority her first concern. "My nephew's hurt. Can I go to him?"

"Why not?" Paula shrugged as Tess sped to where Joey was lying. As she dropped to her knees beside him, the female agent continued talking, but not to her. "As you can see, Arne, Virgil isn't here."

"Obviously." His tone was peevish. "How'd you screw that one up? Is he really on his way like she said?"

Joey's eyes were still closed. Feeling carefully beneath his head, Tess's fingers closed around the small rock that he'd landed on when he'd fallen. Quickly she felt his pulse.

It was a little weaker than it should have been, but still steady enough, she thought with relief. But any loss of consciousness was serious enough to require immediate medical attention. She raised her head as Paula answered the area director's question.

"Sure, Connor's coming. I need him here, Arne. Say, did that tough little Dineh rip your pant leg when he kicked you?"

"I don't think—"

The flat crack of Paula's pistol ripped explosively through the silence of the night. Arne Jansen crumpled bonelessly to the ground. Bending down to pick up the gun that had fallen with him, Paula met Tess's shocked and bewildered gaze.

"No more glass ceiling," she said with a smile. The smile broadened. "Oh, God—you thought I was on your side for a second there, didn't you? You thought I killed the bad guy so we could all go home to the ranch, right?''

"I don't know what to think anymore." Tess shook her head. "Paula, you saved this little boy's life today. I don't know how badly he hurt his head when he fell, but he needs medical attention. I can't believe you'd stand in the way of him getting it."

"This afternoon I needed Joey alive to testify that he'd seen Jansen in that alleyway. I was going to arrange a meeting with Arne all by myself and kill him with no witnesses around. Then I was going to play the big heroine who took down a murderous area director at great risk to her own life, and the organized-crime task force position would have been offered to me on a platter. Jack Vincenzi wouldn't have cared that his partner's second-in-command had just taken over the reins, as long as I was just as willing to be paid off for turning a blind eye as Arne always was.''

Paula tipped her head to one side. "I don't see why it still can't work that way, even though the body count's going to be a little higher."

"You're going to kill me and Joey with his gun, aren't you?" Controlling the tremor in her voice with difficulty, Tess got to her feet. "It's going to look as though your shot took him down just a second too late to prevent his final two murders."

"And this time I don't have to shoot myself in the head to make it look good." Paula grimaced. "My aim was a little off that night, but hell, was I rushed. Hit the lights, shoot Rick, grab Rick's gun, shoot Danzig. Then I had to haul Rick down to the parking garage in the freight elevator, dump him into the trunk of my car, and heave him into the cement I'd seen poured earlier in the day. Good thing I'm not a shortie-pants like you or it would have been beyond me."

"So you never intended to kill Joey that night?" Tess shook her head. "But of course you didn't. You wanted him to testify against Jansen in the future, when you made your play for the task-force position."

"Plus I knew very well that Joey had been climbing around in the air ducts and would be able to escape. He's a toughie, like I keep telling you. I'm not happy about having to kill the two of you, Tess, believe me. I'm not a monster."

"Yes, you are." Tess held Geddes's gaze. "I've seen monsters, so I know what they look like. Most of them look ordinary, like you and Jansen. Some of them look terrifying, like Skinwalker."

She took a shallow breath. "What made you change your mind about letting Joey live, Paula? Or should I say, *who* made you change your mind? Did you meet him on your walk tonight, just before you and I talked in the kitchen? It had to have been sometime after you saved us from the rattler, because he was the one who shut us in there, wasn't he?"

"What the hell are you talking about?" For the first time the female agent's features showed a flash of disconcertion. "Like I said, when I thought Joey could finger Jansen as being with Quayle in the alleyway I wanted him alive, but when I realized he was keeping to his stupid monster story I figured I'd use him as bait instead, to bring Arne here tonight. I told Joey I thought I'd seen Chorrie just past the gate and I knew he'd sneak out of his bed and go looking for him there. Jansen was waiting for him, just like I told him—''

''Tess, get *down!*''

Tess whirled around in shock at the familiar voice coming from beyond the four-by-four—the voice she'd come to know like no other, the voice that belonged to the man she loved. A split second later she attempted to comply with Connor's shouted warning, but it was already too late. Acting instantly Paula yanked her in front of her as a shield. Tess saw Connor's raised gun arm, saw him check the movement of his finger on the trigger, saw his body spin sideways as Paula, Arne Jansen's gun in her hand, fired.

Connor slumped against the side of the four-by-four. Slowly he slid down the body of the vehicle to the ground.

''*Connor!*'' Tess struggled in Paula's grasp, her frozen gaze fixed on the body of the man by the truck. ''Let me *go,* damn you! Let me *go* to him!''

A terrible grief seared through her, and she turned tear-blinded eyes to the woman holding her. ''I *loved* him. You've *killed* him!''

''Of course I did. I told you I was going to. Did you think at the last moment you would whip out your monster-slaying gear and stop me?'' Paula's expression was baffled. ''This is crazy. I think our little conversation is over.''

Roughly she shoved Tess aside and strode over to Joey's unconscious body. She started to raise the gun in her hand.

"No!" The scream ripped from Tess's throat, but even as it left her mouth she heard it overlaid with another, more explosive sound.

As if some giant hand had smashed into her, Paula's body flew backward and landed on the rocks near Joey. In disbelief Tess saw the dark hole in her forehead, just above her wide and lifeless gaze.

"Did…did I get her?"

Connor was raised up on one elbow, his gun still in his hand, but even as she ran to him and knelt beside him, he collapsed to the ground.

"You got her, Connor. She…she's dead. Where did her shot get you?"

"My side," he gasped. "Is Joey all right?"

"He's unconscious. I have to get both of you to a doctor. Can…can you stand?"

"I needed to tell you something." His voice was thick and slurred. "Very…very important."

"Tell me when we get to the clinic in Last Chance," Tess said worriedly. She slung his arm around her shoulder and tried to get him upright. "Right now I have to get you into the truck, Connor."

"I…I see us." With what appeared to be great effort, Connor opened his eyes and held her gaze. "You asked me what I saw earlier. I gave you the wrong answer. I see us, Tess. I see us married and living at the Double B with Joey. I see us making children of our own in time. Do…do you see that?"

His eyes closed. At the side of his throat Tess saw a heavy pulse, still beating, but frighteningly slow.

He'd said he loved her. He'd seen the same future

she'd wanted—the two of them, together with Joey, creating new life.

She had no intention of letting that future slip away.

Joey first, since he was lightest, she thought as she ran to him. She would put him in the four-by-four's back seat, and then somehow get Connor into the front. Then she would drive hell-for-leather to Last—

"You saw me that night, didn't you, Dineh?"

Every hair lifted on the back of Tess's neck. Slowly she rose from Joey's body and stared at the shadowy apparition blocking her way to the four-by-four and Connor.

His voice sounded like stones grating together. She could make out the gleam of a yellow eye, but the rest of him was a block of darkness, as if everything evil in the night had flown together to form him.

"I...I saw you, Skinwalker."

All her life she'd known this moment was coming, she thought light-headedly. Now that the monster was finally before her she knew what she had to do.

This time she had to go up against it and win.

She tried to swallow. "Stand aside and let me be about my business here," she said unsteadily.

"Your business became my business some time ago." The grating voice sounded amused. "The old lady knows that. I don't know how she knows, but she does. The boy dies. The man dies. And you die. It's all part of a bigger picture."

"Then I'm looking at my death." Tess heard the fear in her voice, and tried to control it. "You called me Dineh, so you know I need to prepare myself and the boy.''

As she spoke she raised trembling fingers to her neck, touching the leather thong around it. The figure nodded.

''I respect honor and tradition. Use the pollen.''

''Beauty before me, I walk. Beauty behind me, I walk.''

It wasn't going to work, Tess thought desperately as she intoned the words. He would guess her intentions, would easily thwart them, and after he'd dealt with her he would turn on the two people she loved— the child she'd sworn to protect and the man she'd given her heart to. Who was she to go up against monsters, anyway? What had made her think she had the weapons and the will to take a stand against real evil?

Who are you? The voice in her head sounded incredulous. *You're Dineh. You're the daughter of Dineh, the sister of a courageous Dineh woman, and the aunt of a tough little Dineh boy. And if those alone aren't strength enough, you're a woman in love with a man who was willing to risk his life for you.*

The voice in her head was right, Tess thought slowly as she pulled the thong from around her neck. Her love for Connor had freed her from the pain of the past. His love for her was a shield nothing could destroy. And her heritage had put the weapon she needed right into her hand.

The leather bag came free of her T-shirt. Her voice no longer unsteady, she took up the final few lines of the familiar and comforting chant.

"Beauty above me, I walk. Beauty below me, I walk."

She loosened the neck of the bag. Grasping it with one hand, she spilled a little of the golden pollen into her other palm, and let it drift down onto Joey at her feet.

"Your magic isn't strong enough to put off the inevitable, Dineh." Skinwalker's voice held a note of impatience. "Enough, now. Tell yourself it's a good day to die, and face me."

"Beauty all around me, I walk…" Tess finished softly. Her hand folded over the thin leather bag. Through the thin leather she felt the tiny but deadly purse-gun she'd drawn on Connor at the diner the first time they'd met…the gun she had slipped into the medicine bag before leaving the Double B tonight. She turned to the figure beside the vehicle.

"It's a good day to die, Skinwalker," she said clearly, raising the medicine bag and aiming the tiny derringer through the leather directly at him. "*Your* day, you monster."

Even as the determined words left her lips, she squeezed off the shot.

"*No!*"

The single word slashed through the darkness like a knife as the figure in front of her staggered sideways, a hand to its chest. Around him the night seemed to grow denser, become blacker.

The blackness melted as the road above the gully suddenly became filled with lights and shouting.

"Tess! Connor!"

It was Del's voice, but Jess was the first down the

embankment, Daniel Bird and a big man whom Tess didn't recognize close on Jess's heels.

"We heard shots—"

Jess broke off as his shocked gaze took in the scene—Paula's body lying close to that of Jansen's, an unconscious Connor by the four-by-four, Joey nearby.

"I'll tell Del to phone the clinic in Last Chance on his cell phone, get Doc Jennings to ready his emergency unit for a couple of patients," Daniel said, immediately turning back the way he'd come. "Mac, help me get the stretcher from the truck."

"Three patients," Tess said, feeling a shakiness start somewhere deep inside her. "I don't think my shot killed—"

The words died in her throat as she glanced toward the spot where only a moment ago the enemy she'd fired at had been standing. Now there was no one and nothing there.

"Skinwalker wasn't killed," Joey said faintly, raising his head and gazing at her with dazed eyes. "I saw him run into the shadows, Tess. You kicked his butt good, didn't you? I knew you would."

Tears spilled unheeded down her face as she fell to her knees and gathered him to her. "Don't talk, champ," she said, her words tumbling over one another. "Just take it easy. We're going to get you to a doctor to make sure you're okay."

"Skinwalker?" Joey didn't seem to hear Jess's worried mutter, but it reached Tess's ears. "It's not a good sign if the little guy's hallucinating. How hard did he hit his head—"

"Your trouble is you need proof of something before you'll believe it, Crawford. Problem is, sometimes the proof is all around you, and you won't let yourself see it. I'm just glad I finally figured that one out."

Connor's voice was a thread, but the gaze he directed on Tess as she flew to him was steady and unclouded. "You took on the monster and won, didn't you, sweetheart?" he said softly. "You think for your next assignment you might want to take on a stubborn former FBI agent who's decided to turn rancher?"

Crystal-gray eyes full of love gleamed up at Tess. She felt joyous tears streaming from her own.

"Do you know what the Dineh word *aoo* means, Connor?" She didn't give him the chance to answer, but instead brought her lips to his.

"It means yes," she whispered.

Epilogue

"FBI Agent Turns Down Promotion, Weds Alien-Hunter and Moves to Ranch." The woman in front of Tess and Joey and Connor in the grocery checkout line extracted the tabloid from the magazine rack beside her and sniffed. "Oh, for heaven's sakes. Who believes these things?"

"I do," Tess whispered to Connor. "Ever since you whisked me and Joey off to Vegas a couple of weeks ago and we got married by that minister turned Elvis impersonator, that is. How 'bout you?"

"I think I started believing it when I was being held at gunpoint in a cheap motel by a crazy lady," he said, pulling her to him and dropping a quick kiss on the tip of her nose.

"And I believed it when Del said that if we're going to be living at the Double B from now on, I should have my own horse," Joey grinned. "Tess, I'm going to run out to the car and make sure Chorrie's not too hot. I know we left the windows rolled down, but he might need a drink."

"Okay." Tess smiled up at Connor as the nine-year-old tore out of the grocery store. "You know, I bet I can guess what the *Eye-Opener*'s headline's going to be next week. If the guys on the paper decide to play another trick on me and use my life for inspiration again, of course.''

"What's that?'' Connor ruffled her hair.

She lifted herself on her tiptoe and whispered something in his ear. She stood back and waited for his response.

"You mean we're...you're really—'' Slow joy spread across his features. "That's *unbelievable!*''

"That's what I say, too,'' said the woman ahead of them with a sniff, as she added the tabloid to her groceries.

But Virgil Connor's brand-new wife, Tess, didn't hear the sniffed comment.

She was too busy being kissed by her unborn baby's father.

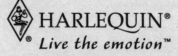

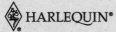

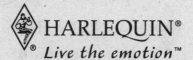

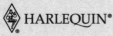

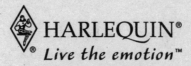